"Look at me, Lizzy."

Gabe was asking a lot, considering how tumultuous Elizabeth's emotions were at the moment. It took several seconds for her to finally comply.

He was breathing roughly. "I don't know what it is about you, Red, but you make me feel like I'm going to explode." His hot fingers moved on her thigh, making her breath catch. "Have you ever played baseball?"

She blinked. "I...no."

Gabe nodded. "I'll teach you baseball, but not the kind you're thinking of."

He bent his golden head and pressed a soft, damp kiss onto her knee. "I think we'll just try first base tonight. If you like it, then tomorrow at the drive-in, we'll go to second base. Do you understand?"

"I think so." Her throat felt raw, but then she had a gorgeous hunk of man kneeling at her feet, staring at her with lust. "Is what you're doing now considered first base?"

Very slowly, Gabe shook his head. "No, this is just me, torturing myself."

Dear Reader,

As I wrote Gabe's story, in my mind I revisited Kentucky
and the small family cottage we have on a lake there.
The best summers of my life were spent swimming
and waterskiing and sunning myself. Like Gabe, I'm
something of a water baby. I learned to ski when I was
six, and I can't remember a time when I wasn't able to
swim. Put me near water and I'm happy. I love the heat
and I'm miserable in the cold.

Whenever I get mind weary, I can go to the cottage
and worries just seem to evaporate. I personally
believe that's by nature's design. The combination of
slight breezes, leaves rustling, birds and fish and bright
sunshine, and especially the lulling of water lapping at
the shore is, in my mind, conducive to pleasure—and
romance. This was, by far, my favorite book in the series
to write. I hope it can take you away, as it did me.

And I hope, like me, you have a special place you can
visit that helps soothe you when you need it most.

Take care, have a wonderful summer and don't miss
Jordan's story—the last in THE BUCKHORN BROTHERS
series—coming in September.

Lori Foster

P.S. You can write to me at P.O. Box 854, Ross, Ohio,
45061

Books by Lori Foster

HARLEQUIN TEMPTATION
786—SAWYER*
790—MORGAN*

*The Buckhorn Brothers

Lori Foster
GABE

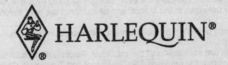

HARLEQUIN®

TORONTO • NEW YORK • LONDON
AMSTERDAM • PARIS • SYDNEY • HAMBURG
STOCKHOLM • ATHENS • TOKYO • MILAN • MADRID
PRAGUE • WARSAW • BUDAPEST • AUCKLAND

To my son, Mason

If we could bottle your endless energy,
we'd make a fortune! You're fearless,
always ready to shake things up and you've never
met a stranger, because you make them all friends.
There's nothing you can't do when you set your mind
to it, which you do, more often than not.
I hope the world is ready for you, because I know
you're ready for the world.
I love you, Mason, very much.

ISBN 0-373-25894-1

GABE

Copyright © 2000 by Lori Foster

1

"Isn't he just the absolute sexiest thing you've ever seen?"

"Hmm. And thank heavens for this heat wave. I love it when he leaves his shirt off." A wistful, feminine sigh. "I swear, I could sit here all day and look at him."

"We *have* been sitting here all day looking at him."

Gabe Kasper, pretending to be asleep, had to struggle with a small smile. Life was good. Here he was, sprawled in the warm sun, letting the waves from the weekend boaters gently rock the dock, with a fishing pole loosely held in one hand, a Van Halen hat pulled low over his eyes and a gaggle of good-lookin' women ogling him. He had not a care in the world. Man couldn't ask for much more satisfaction out of living.

"He is *so* gorgeous."

"And wicked lookin'. I dearly love those whiskers on his chin."

Aha. And here his brother Jordan had sworn the whiskers looked disreputable and tried to convince him to shave. Jordan could be such a stuffed shirt sometimes.

"I like that golden hair on his body, myself."

Gabe almost chuckled out loud. He couldn't wait to

tell his brothers about this. Now that the two eldest were married and off-limits, Gabe and Jordan, the only two single ones left, got even more attention. Not that he was complaining. Female adoration was one of those things that couldn't really go to excess, at least, in his opinion.

"I don't mind tellin' you, Rosemary, it made me nervous when the first two brothers got married off. I cried for two days, and I was so afraid they'd all end up doing it. Heck, besides dying to have one of them to myself, those brothers were the biggest tourist draw we had here in Buckhorn."

Gabe bit the side of his lip. He'd just keep that little tidbit to himself when he did the retelling. Hell, his brothers' egos—Morgan's especially—were big enough as it was. No need adding to them. No, he'd just stick to sharing the compliments about himself.

"And Gabe is the biggest draw my boat dock has. With him sitting there, no one wants to get their gas or bait anywhere else. I keep thinkin' I ought to pay him or something."

"Ha! You're just hoping to get a little closer to him."

"No, I just wanna make sure he doesn't take his sexy self off to some other dock."

"Amen to that!"

Giggles erupted after such a heartfelt comment and Gabe sighed. He had no intention of switching loyalties. Hell, Rosemary's daddy had been letting him hang out on his docks since he was just a grasshopper and had first noticed what a pleasing thing it was to see females in bikinis. This place felt almost like a second home now. And since Rosemary's daddy had passed away, he felt honor bound to stick around and help out on occasion. The trick was to keep Rosemary from getting marriage minded, because that was one route his brothers could travel alone, thank you very much.

"It amazes me that those brothers aren't full related. They all look different—"

"But they're all gorgeous, I know. And they're all so...*strong*. My daddy used to say it took a hell of a woman to raise boys like that. I just wish they didn't live so far out on that land. Thinking up a good excuse to visit isn't easy. Not like accidentally running into the other men here in town."

Gabe did smile at that, he couldn't help himself. He and his brothers—he refused to think of them as half brothers—had often joked about going into town to see who was looking for them. Usually some female or another was. But by living out a ways, they could always choose when and if they wanted to get friendly. It had been helpful, because once they'd hit their teens, the females had come on in droves. His mother used to claim to keep a broom by the front and back doors to beat the women away. Not that any of them minded overmuch, though his two new sisters-in-law were sure disgruntled over all the downcast female faces since the two weddings had taken place.

Gabe was just about to give up feigning sleep when a new female voice joined the others over by the gas pumps.

"Excuse me, but I was told Gabriel Kasper might

be here." It was more a statement than anything else, and rather...strident to boot.

Female, but not at all local.

This new voice wasn't soft, Southern or sweet. She'd sounded almost impatient.

Gabe decided just to wait and see what the lady was up to. It wasn't unusual for someone female to be looking for him, and most everyone in these parts knew that in the summer, you could find him by the lake more often than not. He resisted the urge to peek at the owner of the voice and kept his body utterly relaxed.

"Whatdya want Gabe for?" That suspicious tone was from Rosemary, bless her sweet little heart, and Gabe vowed to take her to dinner real soon.

There was a beat of silence, then, "I have personal business to discuss with him."

Oh, great, Gabe thought. That'll get the gossip going. What the hell kind of personal business could he have with a woman he didn't know? And he was certain he didn't know her. She didn't sound at all familiar.

"Well, he's right there, but he's relaxin', and he won't thank you none for disturbing him."

"I appreciate your warning."

Well used to the soft thud of sneakers or bare feet on the wooden planks of the dock, Gabe almost winced when the clack of hard-soled shoes rang over the water. He ignored it, and ignored the woman he could feel hesitating next to his lawn chair. The breeze stirred and he caught a light feminine scent, not really perfume, but maybe scented shampoo. He breathed deeply, but otherwise remained still.

He heard her clear her throat. "Uh...excuse me?"

She didn't sound so confident, and he waited, wondering if she'd shake him awake. He felt her hesitate, knew in his gut she was reaching for his naked shoulder...

And the fishing pole nearly leaped out of his hand.

"Son of a bi—" Gabe jolted upright, barely managing to hang on to his expensive rod and reel. His feet hit the dock and he deftly maneuvered the rod, going with the action of the fish. "Damn, it's a big one!"

Rosemary, Darlene and Ceily all ran over to his side.

"I'll grab the net!" Rosemary said.

Ceily, who usually worked the diner in town, squealed as the fish, a big ugly carp, flipped up out the water. Darlene pressed to his back, peering over his shoulder.

Gabe slid over the side of the dock to the smooth, slick, moss-covered concrete boat ramp, bracing his legs wide to keep his balance while he struggled with the fish. Rosemary, a fisherwoman of long standing, didn't hesitate to slip in beside him. She held the net at the ready. Just as Gabe got the carp close enough, she scooped him with the net. The fish looked to weigh a good fifteen pounds, and she struggled with it while Gabe tried to reach for the net and hold onto his pole.

But then Rosemary lost her footing and Gabe made a grab for her and they both went down, splashing and cursing and laughing, too. The rod jerked out of his hands and he dove forward to grab it, barely getting ahold and soaking himself thoroughly in the process. The other two women leaped in to help, all of them struggling to keep the fish and the rod while roaring with hilarity.

When the battle was over, Gabe had his fish, and a woman, in his lap. Rosemary had settled herself there while Darlene and Ceily hung on him, both struggling to control their raucous laughter. He'd known all three of them since grade school, so it wasn't the first time they'd played in the water; they felt totally familiar with each other and it showed. A long string of seaweed clung to the top of Gabe's head, and that started the women giggling again.

Gabe, enjoying himself, unhooked the big fish, kissed it—making the women smack at him—then tossed it back.

It was then they heard the tap, tap, tap of that damned hard-soled shoe.

Turning as one, they all peered at the woman who Gabe only then remembered. He had to shade his eyes against the hot sun to see, and it wasn't easy with three women draped over his body.

Silhouetted by the sunshine, her long hair looked like ruby fire. And he'd never in his life seen so many freckles on a woman before. She wore a crisp white blouse, a long jean skirt and black pumps with nylons. *Nylons in this heat?* Gabe blinked. "Can I help you with somethin', sugar?"

Her lips tightened and her arms crossed over her

middle. "I don't think so. I was looking for Gabriel Kasper."

"That'd be me."

"But...I was looking for Gabriel, the town hero."

Darlene grinned hugely. "That's our Gabe!"

Ceily added, "The one and only."

Gabe rolled his eyes. "That's nonsense and you all know it."

The women all started in at once, Ceily, Rosemary and Darlene assuring him he was all that was heroic and wonderful and more.

Little Red merely stared in absolute disbelief. "You mean, *you* are the one who rescued those swimmers?"

He gently lifted Rosemary off his lap and cautiously stood on the slick concrete. The women had gone silent now, and Gabe could see why. While they looked downright sexy in their colorful bikinis, loose hair and golden tans, this woman looked like the stern, buttoned-up supervisor of a girls' prep school. And she was glaring at them all, as if she'd caught them having an orgy in the lake, rather than just romping.

Gabe, always the gentleman, boosted each woman to the dock, then deftly hauled himself out. He shook like a mongrel dog, sending lake water flying in cold droplets. The woman quickly backed up two steps.

Rosemary plucked the seaweed from his hair and he grinned at her. "Thanks, sweetie. Ah, would you gals mind if I talk to..." He lifted a brow at Red.

"Elizabeth Parks," she answered stiffly. She clutched a notepad and pencil and had a huge purse-like bag slung over one shoulder, stuffed to overflowing with papers.

"Yeah, can I have a minute with Ms. Parks?" He had the sneaking suspicion Ms. Parks was another reporter, and he had no intention of chatting with her for more time than it took to say thanks but no thanks. "I won't be long."

"All right, Gabe, but you owe us for rescuing your fish."

"That I do. And I promise to think up some appropriate compensation."

Giggling again, the women started away, dragging their feet every step, sashaying their sexy behinds. But then two boats pulled in and he knew that would keep them busy selling gas and bait and whatever other supplies the vacationers wanted. He turned to Red.

"What can I do for you?"

Now, without the sun in his eyes, Gabe could see she had about the bluest blue eyes he'd ever seen. They stood out like beacons among all that bright red hair and those abundant freckles.

She flipped open her bag and dragged out a folded newspaper. Turning it toward him, she asked, still with a twinge of disbelief, "Is this you?"

She sounded suspicious, but Gabe didn't even have to glance at the paper. Buckhorn, Kentucky was a small town, and they looked for any excuse at all to celebrate. The town paper, *Buckhorn Press*, had used the changing of a traffic light for front-page news once, so it was no wonder they'd stuck him in there for a spell when he helped fish a few swimmers out of the path of an unmanned boat. It hadn't been even close to an act of heroism, but if changing traffic lights was important, human endangerment was outright momentous.

"Yeah, that's me." Gabe reached for his mirrored sunglasses and slipped them on, then dragged both hands, fingers spread, over his head to smooth his wet hair. He stuck his cap on backward then looked at the woman again. With the shades in place, he could check her over a little better without her knowing.

But the clothing she wore made seeing much impossible. She had to be roasting in that thick denim and starched cotton.

She cleared her throat. "Well, if it's really true, then I'd like to interview you."

Gabe leaned around her, which made her blue eyes widen, and fetched a can of cola from the cooler sitting beside his empty chair. "You want one?"

"Uh, no, thank you." She hastily stepped back, avoiding getting too close to him. That nettled.

After popping the tab on the can and downing half of it, Gabe asked, "What paper do you write for?"

"Oh. No, I don't—"

"Because I'm not interested in being interviewed again. Every damn paper for a hundred miles around picked up on that stupid story, and they blew it all out of proportion. Folks around here are finally about done razzing me, my damn brothers included, and I'm not at all interested in resurrecting that ridiculous business again."

She frowned at him, then snapped the paper open

to peruse it. "Did you or did you not dive into the water to pull three people, a woman and her two children, out of the lake when a drunken man fell out of his boat, leaving the boat unmanned?"

Gabe made a face. "Yeah, but—"

"No one else did anything, they just sort of stood there dumbfounded while the boat, without a driver, began circling the hapless swimmers."

"Hapless swimmers?" He grunted at her word usage. "Any one of my brothers would have done the exact same thing, and in fact—"

"And did you or did you not then manage to get in the boat—" She glanced up. "I'd love for you to explain how you did that, by the way. How you took control and got inside a running boat without getting chewed to bits by the prop. Weren't you at all scared?"

Gabe stared at her. Even her lashes were reddish, sort of a deep auburn, and with the sun on them, the tips were turned to gold. She squinted against the glare of the sunshine, which made the freckles on her tipped-up nose more pronounced. Other than those sprinkled freckles, her skin was smooth and clear and...

He shook himself. "Look, sugar, I said I didn't want to do an interview."

She puckered up like someone had stuck a lemon between her lips. "My name is Ms. Parks, or Elizabeth, either will do, thank you." After that reprimand, she had the audacity to say, "All the others wanted to be interviewed. Why don't you?"

She stood there, slim brows raised, her pencil

poised over that damn notepad as if she expected to write down his every profound word.

Gabe cursed. Profound words were not his forté. They took too much effort. "What others?"

"The other heroes."

He could see her long hair curling in the humidity even as they spoke. It hung almost to the top of her behind, except for the front which was pulled back with a huge barrette. Little wispy curls, dark with perspiration, clung to her temples. The longer hair was slowly pulling into corkscrew curls. It fascinated him.

The front of her white blouse was beginning to grow damp, too, and Gabe could detect a plain white bra beneath. Damn, it was too hot to be all trussed up like that. What the hell kind of rigid female wore so many clothes to a vacation lake during the most sweltering heat wave of the summer season?

He didn't care what kind of female. "All right, first things first. I'm not doing any interview, period. Two, I'll admit I'm curious as to what the hell you're talking about with this other heroes business. And three, would you be more comfortable in the shade? Your face is turning berry red."

If anything, her color intensified. It wasn't exactly a pretty blush, more like someone had set a fire beneath her skin. She looked downright blotchy. Gabe almost laughed.

"I, ah, I always turn red," she explained, somewhat flustered. "Sorry. Redheads have fair skin."

"And you sure as certain have redder hair than most."

"Yes, I'm aware of that."

She looked stiff, as if he'd insulted her. It wasn't like her red hair was a state secret! A body could see that hair from a mile away.

He had to struggle to keep from grinning. "So whatdya say? You wanna go sit in the shade with me? There's a nice big piss elm hanging over the water there and it's cooler than standing here on the dock in the sun, but not much."

She blinked owlishly at him. "A what elm?"

"Piss elm. Just sorta means a scraggly one. Come on." She looked ready to expire on him, from flustered embarrassment, heat and exasperation. Without waiting for her agreement, he grabbed his cooler, took her arm in a firm grip and led her off the dock, over the rough rock retaining wall and through the grass. One large root of the elm stuck out smoothly from the ground and made a nice seat. Gabe practically shoved her onto it. He was afraid she might faint on him any minute. "Rest there a second while I get you a soda."

She scrambled to smooth her skirt over her legs, covering as much skin as possible, while trying to balance her notepad and adjust her heavy purse. "No, thank you. Really, I just—"

He'd already opened a can. "Here, drink up." He shoved the drink into her hand and then waited until she dutifully sipped. "Feel better?"

"Uh, yes, thank you."

She acted so wary, he couldn't help but be curious about her. She wasn't his type—too pushy, too prim, too...*red*. But that didn't mean he'd let her roast herself in the sun. His mother would hide him if she thought he'd been rude to a lady, any lady. Besides, she was kinda cute with her prissiness. In a red sort of way.

Gabe grabbed another cola for himself, then sat on the cooler. He looked at her while he drank. "So, tell me about these heroes."

She carefully licked her lips then set the can in the grass before facing him. "I'm working on a thesis for college. I've interviewed about a half dozen different men who were recently commended for performing heroic acts. So far, they've all had similar personality types. But you—"

"No fooling? What type of personality do heroes have?"

"Well, before I tell you that, I'd like to ask you a few questions. I don't want your answers to be biased by what the others have said."

Gabe frowned, propping his elbows on his knees and glaring at her. "You think I'd lie?"

She rushed to reassure him. "No! Not consciously. But just to keep my study pure, I'd rather conduct all the interviews the same way."

"But I've already told you, I don't want to be interviewed." He watched her closely, saw her frustration and accurately guessed that wasn't typical behavior of a hero. *What nonsense.*

After a long minute, she said, "Okay, can I ask you something totally different?"

"Depends. Ask, then I'll see if I want to answer."

"Why'd you throw the fish back?"

Gabe looked over his shoulder to where he'd caught the carp, then back. "That fish I just caught?"

"Yes. Why fish if you're not going to keep what you catch."

He chuckled. "You don't get out by the lake much, do you?"

"I'm actually not from around here. I'm just visiting the area—"

"To interview me?" The very idea floored him, and made him feel guilty for giving her such a hard time.

"Yes, actually." She took another drink of the soda, then added, "I rented a place and I'm staying for the month until school starts back up. I wanted to have all my research together before then. I'd thought I was done, and I was due a short vacation, but then I read the papers about you and decided to add one more interview."

"So you're working during your vacation?" He snorted. That was plain nuts. Vacations were for relaxing, and the idea of wasting one to pester him didn't make sense.

"Yes, well, let's just say that, hopefully, I'm combining my vacation with an interview. I couldn't resist. Your situation was unique in that every time you were quoted, you talked about someone else."

"I remember." The people he'd talked about were more interesting than anything he had to say about himself.

"You went on and on about how brave the two little kids were..."

"They were real sweet kids, and—"

"...and you lectured something fierce about drinking and water sports."

"This is a dry lake, which means no alcohol. That damn fool who fell out of his boat could have killed someone."

She gave him a coy look, surprising the hell out of him with the natural sensuality of it. She was so starchy, he hadn't been at all prepared. "But you keep saying the situation wasn't dangerous."

"It wasn't. Not to me." She looked smug, and she wrote something on her paper, making him frown. He decided to explain before she got the wrong idea. "Hell, I've been swimming like a fish since I was still in diapers. I was in this lake before I could walk. My brothers taught me to water-ski when I was barely five years old, and I know boats inside and out. There was no risk to me at all, so there's no way anyone in their right mind can label me a hero."

"So you say. But everyone else seems to disagree."

"Sweetheart, you just don't know Buckhorn. This town is so settled and quiet, any disturbance at all is fodder for front-page news. Why, we had a cow break out of the pasture and wander into the church-yard sometime back. Stopped traffic for miles around so everyone could gawk. The fire department showed up, along with my brother, who's the sheriff, and the *Buckhorn Press* sent all their star reporters to cover the story."

"All their star reporters?"

He grinned. "Yeah. All two of them. That's the way things are run around here. The town council meets to vote on whether or not to change the bulbs in the street lamps and last year when Mrs. Rommen's kitty went missing, a search party was formed and we hunted for three days before finding the old rascal."

She wrote furiously, which annoyed the hell out of Gabe, and then she looked up. "We?"

He tilted his head at her teasing smile, a really nice smile now that he was seeing it. Her lips were full and rosy and... He frowned. "Now, Ms. Parks, you wouldn't expect me to avoid my civic duty, would you? Especially not when the old dear loves that ugly tomcat something fierce."

She grinned at him again, putting dimples in those abundant freckles, making her wide mouth even more appealing, before going back to her writing. Gabe leaned forward to see exactly what she was putting on paper, and she snatched the paper to her chest.

"What are you doing?" She sounded breathless and downright horrified.

Gabe lifted a brow. "Just peeking at what you consider so noteworthy."

"Oh, I'm sorry." She lowered the paper, but the damage had been done. Dark smears of pencil lead were etched across the front of her damp white blouse.

Gabe nodded appreciatively at her bosom while sipping his cola. "Looks like you'll need to be cleaned up." He said it, then stood. "You should probably head on home to do that."

She quickly stood, too. "But I haven't asked you my questions yet."

"And you won't. I don't want to be interviewed.

But just for the hell of it, I turned the fish loose 'cause it's a carp, not that good for eating and a real pain to clean being as they have a mud vein. Bass is more to my tastes. Which doesn't matter any when you're fishing just for the fun of fishing, which is usually how I do it. You should try it sometime." He looked her over slowly. "Cuttin' loose, I mean. It's real relaxing."

He turned to walk away and she trotted to keep up with him. "Gabriel...Mr. Kasper..."

"Gabe will do, unless you're thinking to ask more questions." He said it without looking at her, determined to get away before he noticed anything about her besides her lips, which now that he'd noticed he couldn't stop noticing, or how nicely that starched shirt was beginning to stick to her breasts in the humidity. He still couldn't tell for sure, but he suspected a slight possibility that she was built rather nice beneath all the prim, stiff clothing. And that was the kind of suspicion that could distract a man something awful.

Only she wasn't the kind of woman he wanted to be distracted by. She had an obvious agenda, while he avoided plans and merely enjoyed each day.

"Gabe, really, this isn't a lengthy interview. There's no reason for you to be coy."

He had to laugh at that. Shaking his head, he stepped on the dock and looked at her. He could have sworn he saw another long red tress snap into a curl right before his eyes. Her whole head was beginning to look like corkscrews. Long, lazy, red corkscrews. It was kinda cute in a way... Hell, no. No, it was not cute.

"I've never been called *coy* in my life. I'm just plain not interested in that foolishness." He skimmed off his sunglasses and hat, and placed them on his chair, then tossed a fat inflated black inner tube into the lake. "Now, I'm going to go cool off with a dip. You can either skim out of those clothes and join me before you expire from the heat, or you can go find some other fool to interview. But no more questions." He started to turn away, but belatedly added, "Nice meeting you." Then he dove in.

He was sure his splash got her, but he didn't look to see. At least not at first.

She stood there for the longest time. He was strangely aware of her presence while he hoisted himself into the center of the inner tube and got comfortable. Peeking through one eye, he watched her stew in silence, then glare at him before marching off.

Finally. Let her leave.

Calling him a hero—what nonsense. His brothers were real heroes; even those kids that had kept their cool and not whined could be considered heroic little devils. But not Gabe Kasper. No, sir.

He started to relax, tipping his head into the cool water to drench his hair and lazily drifting his arms. But his neck snapped to attention when he saw Little Red stop beside Rosemary. She pointed at Gabe, then pulled out her damn notepad when Rosemary began chattering. And damn if Ceily and Darlene didn't wander closer, taking part.

Well, hell. She was gossiping about him!

When he'd told her to interview someone else, he meant someone else who wouldn't talk about him. Someone not on the lake. Hell, someone not even in Buckhorn—not even in Kentucky!

Rosemary's mouth was going a mile a minute, and he could only imagine what was being said. He ground his teeth in frustration.

A couple of women in a docked boat started flirting with him, but Gabe barely noticed. He stared at Rosemary, trying to will her to clam up, but not wanting to appear too concerned about the whole thing. What was it with Red, that she'd be so damn pushy? He'd explained he wasn't a hero, that she didn't need him for her little survey or whatever it was she conducted. But could she let that go? Hell, no.

One of the women from the docked boat—a really nice inboard that cost more than some houses—dove in and swam over to him. Gabe sent her a distracted smile.

It was in his nature to flirt; he just couldn't seem to help himself, and he'd never yet met a woman who minded. This particular woman didn't. She took his smile as an invitation.

Yet anytime he'd gotten even remotely close to Red, she'd frozen up like he was a big water snake ready to take a bite. Obviously she wanted into his head, but nowhere else.

Strange woman.

She walked away from Rosemary with a friendly wave, and Gabe started to breathe a sigh of relief— until she stopped a few yards up the incline where Bear, the repairman who worked on boat engines for

Rosemary, was hanging around. Gabe helped the man regularly, whenever things got too busy, but did Bear remember that now? Gabe snorted. The old whiskered cuss looked at Red warily, then glanced at Gabe, and a smile as wide as the dam spread across his wrinkled face. Just that fast, Little Red had her pencil racing across the paper again.

"Damn it." Gabe deftly tipped the inner tube and slid over the side into the water. The sudden chill did nothing to cool his simmering temper. Keeping his gaze on the meddling female, he swam—dragging the inner tube—to the dock. But just as he reached it, so did the woman from the boat.

"Ah, now you're not planning to leave just when I got here, are you?"

Gabe turned. He'd actually forgotten the woman, which was incredible. She stood waist deep in the shallow water and from what he could see, she was built like a Barbie doll, all long limbs and long blond hair, and so much cleavage, she fairly overflowed her skimpy bikini bra. She should have held all his attention, but instead, he'd been thoroughly distracted by an uptight, overly freckled, redheaded wonder of a woman who jumped if he even looked at her.

Gabe glanced at Red, and their gazes clashed. He'd thought to go set the little darling straight on how much prying he'd put up with, but he reconsidered.

Oh, she was in a hot temper. Her blue-eyed gaze was glued to him, and her pencil was thankfully still. It was then Gabe realized his female swimming companion had caught hold of his arm—and Red disapproved mightily. She was looking like a schoolmarm again, all rigid, her backbone straight. Well, now. That was more like it.

Gabe turned to the blonde with a huge smile. This might just turn out to be fun.

2

ELIZABETH narrowed her eyes as she watched Gabriel Kasper fairly ooze masculine charm over the woman draped at his side. And the woman *was* draped. Elizabeth snorted in disgust. Did all women want to hang on him? Rosemary, Darlene, Ceily and this woman. They seemed to come from all around just to coo at him. No wonder he seemed so...different from the others.

The men she'd interviewed so far had been full of ego over their heroics and more than willing to share their stories with any available ear. They were rightfully proud, considering they'd behaved in a brave, out of the ordinary way that had directly benefited the people around them. Some of them had been shy, some outrageous, but not a one of them had refused her an interview. And not a one of them had so thoroughly ignored her.

No, they'd hung on her every question, anxious to share the excitement, thrilled with her interest, but in a purely self-satisfying way. They certainly hadn't been distracted with her as a woman, eyeing her up and down the way Gabriel Kasper had. She wondered if he thought she was stupid, or just naive, considering the way he'd looked at her, like he thought she wouldn't notice just because he wore sunglasses.

Not likely! She'd felt his gaze like a tactile stroke, and it had unnerved her. The average man just didn't look at her that way, and men like Gabe never gave her a thought.

But then Gabe had dismissed her, and that she was more than used to. Except with the heroes she'd interviewed, the men who wanted their unique stories told.

Damn, Mr. Kasper was an enigma.

"Don't mind that none, miss. Gabe always gets more'n his share of notice from the fillies."

Elizabeth snapped her attention to Bear. His name suited him, she thought, as she looked way, way up into his grizzled face. "I beg your pardon?"

He nodded toward the docks, where Gabe and the woman were chatting cozily. Elizabeth curled her lip. It was disgusting for a woman to put on such an absurd display, especially right out in the open like that. And for Gabe to encourage her so... Good grief, he had a responsibility to the community as a role model after all the attention they'd given him.

"Has he acted any different since becoming a town hero?" During her research, Elizabeth had discovered that people heralded for valor quickly adapted to all the fanfare and added interest thrown their way.

Bear chuckled. "Not Gabe. Truth is, folks in these parts have pretty much always looked up to him and his brothers. I don't think anyone doubted Gabe would do something once he noticed what had happened. Any one of his brothers would have done the same."

"He mentioned his brothers. Can you tell me something about them?"

"Be glad to!" Bear mopped a tattered bandanna around his face, then stuck it in his back pocket. "The oldest brother, Sawyer, is the town doc, and a damn good one to boot. He takes care of everyone from the newborns to the elders. Got hisself married to Honey, a real sweet little woman, about a year back. And that cut his patient load down considerable like. Seems some of the womenfolk coming to see him weren't really sick, just ambitious."

Bear grinned, but Elizabeth shook her head in exasperation.

"Right after Sawyer is Morgan, the sheriff, who generally looks like he just crawled right off a cactus, but he's as nice as they come as long as you stay on his good side." He leaned close to whisper, "And folks in these parts definitely stay on his good side."

"Lovely." Elizabeth tried to picture these two respectable men related to Gabe, who looked like a beach bum, but she couldn't quite manage it.

"Morgan up and married Honey's sister, Misty, just a bit after Sawyer married. He smiles more these days—that is, when she doesn't have him in a temper. She does seem to enjoy riling that boy."

It was a sure sign of Bear's age that he'd call a man older than Gabe a boy.

"Then there's Jordan, the best damn vet Buckhorn County has to offer. He can sing to an animal, and damned if it won't sing back! That man can charm a bird out of a tree or lull an ornery mule asleep. He's still a bachelor."

Good grief. Elizabeth could do no more than blink. Doctor, sheriff, vet. It was certainly an impressive family. "What does Gabe do for a living?"

Bear scratched beneath his chin, thinking, and then he looked away. "Thing is, Gabe's the youngest, and he don't yet know what it is he wants to do. Mostly he's a handyman, sort of a jack-of-all-trades. That boy can do just about anything with his hands. He's—"

"He doesn't have a job?" Elizabeth didn't mean to sound so shocked, but Rosemary had told her Gabe was twenty-seven years old, and to Elizabeth's mind, that was plenty old enough to have figured out your life's ambition.

"Well..."

She shook her head, cutting off whatever lame excuses Bear was prepared to make. "I got the impression from a few things Rosemary said that he worked here."

A cold, wet hand clamped onto her shoulder, and Elizabeth jumped, then whirled to see Gabe, dripping lake water, standing right behind her. His grin wasn't pleasant, and she wished that she hadn't gotten engrossed in what Bear had to say, that she'd kept at least part of her attention on Gabe.

She looked around him, but his newest female companion was nowhere to be found. Which, she supposed, accounted for his presence. Surely if any other woman was available he'd still be ignoring her.

Gabe nodded to Bear, more or less dismissing him, then pulled Elizabeth around and started walking a few feet away. In a voice that only barely bordered on cordial, he said, "Well, Miss Nosy, I do work here, but I'm not employed here. There's a definite difference. And from now on, I'd appreciate it if you kept your questions to yourself. I don't much like people prying into my personal life, especially when I already told 'em not to."

Elizabeth gulped. No amount of forced pleasantness could mask his irritation. She tried to inch away from his hot, controlling grasp, but he wasn't letting go. So she simply stopped.

Gabe turned to face her. They were once again standing in the bright sun, on a gravel drive that declined down the slight hill, used to launch boats into the lake. The glare off the white gravel was blinding. She had to shield her eyes with one hand while balancing her notepad, pen and purse with the other. Looking directly at him both flustered and annoyed her. He was an incredibly...*potent* male, no denying that. Standing there in nothing more than wet, worn, faded cutoffs—and those hanging entirely too low on his lean hips—he was a devastatingly masculine sight. A sparse covering of light brown hair, damp from his swim, laid over solid muscles in his chest and down his abdomen, then swirled around his navel. He was deeply tanned, his legs long, his big feet bare. He seemed impervious to the sharp gravel and the hot sun. And as she watched, his arms crossed over his chest.

"You be sure and let me know when you're done looking so I can finish telling you what I think of your prying ways."

The heat that washed over her face had nothing to

do with the summer sun and everything to do with humiliation.

"I'm sorry. It's just that you don't look like the other men."

He sighed dramatically. "I take it we're talking about the other supposed heroes?"

"Yes."

"And how did they look?"

Elizabeth hesitated, wondering how to explain it. She couldn't just say they had all been fully dressed, because thinking it made her blush more. At the moment, Gabe Kasper looked more naked than not, and even the jean shorts didn't help, considering they were soaked and clinging to his hard thighs, to his... *Don't go there.*

She cleared her throat. "They were all more...serious. They have careers they take great pride in, and they enjoyed telling their stories."

"But I told you, I don't have a story to tell."

"Your friends disagree."

His arms dropped and he scowled at her. Strangely, Elizabeth noticed he was watching her mouth instead of looking into her eyes. It made it easier for her because staring directly at him kept her edgy for some reason. There was so much expression in his eyes, as if he wasn't just looking at her, but really seeing her. It was an unusual experience for her.

But with him looking at her mouth, she felt nervous in a different way, and without thinking, she licked her lips. His gaze shot to hers, and he stared, eyes narrowed, for two heartbeats while she held her breath and felt faint for some stupid reason. She gulped air and fanned her burning face.

Relaxing slightly, he shook his head, then said, "Look, Lizzy—"

"Don't call me that. My name is Elizabeth."

"And as long you're disregarding my wishes, I think I'll just disregard yours. Besides, Lizzy sorta suits you. It sounds like the proper name for a red-haired girl."

Elizabeth wanted to smack him. But since he'd come right out and all but admitted he wanted to annoy her, she decided to deny him the satisfaction. When she remained silent, he smiled, then continued. "This is all foolishness. Now I'm asking you nicely to let it drop."

"I can't. I've decided you'll make a really good contrast to the other men in my study. See, you're very different, and I can't, in good conscience, leave out such an important factor in my study. In order for the study to be accurate, I need to take data from every angle—"

He raised a hand, looking annoyed enough for his head to explode. "Enough of that already. This is your summer break, right?"

She watched him cautiously. "Yes."

"So why work so damn hard on summer break? Why not just cut loose a little and have some fun before going back to school?" He looked her over again and judging by the tightness of his mouth and the expression in his eyes, obviously found her lacking. "You're so prissed up, you have to be sweltering. No one puts on that many clothes in this heat."

Her shoulders were so stiff they hurt, and her stomach was churning. How dare he attack her on such a personal level? "Obviously someone does. I consider my dress totally appropriate."

"Appropriate to what?"

"To interviewing a hero."

His head dropped forward and he groaned. "You are the most stubbornest damn woman...."

"Me? You're the one who refuses to answer a few simple questions."

Their voices had risen and Gabe, with a heartfelt sigh, took her arm again and started farther up the gravel drive.

"Where are we going?" She had a vague image of him dragging her off and wringing her neck. Even a hero could only be pushed so far, and with the way everyone worshiped him, she didn't think she'd get much help.

"We're drawing attention and it isn't the kind of attention I like."

With a sneer she couldn't quite repress, she asked, "You mean it isn't purely female?"

Glancing her way, he grinned. "That's right."

"Oh, for heaven's sake!"

"Here we go. Have a seat."

Luckily, this time it wasn't a root he wanted to perch her on. The rough wooden picnic table was located beneath a tree—not an elm—and though it was partially covered with dried leaves, acorns and twigs, it was at least shaded.

Elizabeth had barely gotten herself settled before

Gabe blurted, "Okay, what is it going to take to get you to back off?"

He wanted to bargain with her? Surprised, but also hopeful because she really did want to add his story to the others—he was proving to be the exception that broke the hero mold she'd mentally formed—Elizabeth carefully considered her answer. Finally, she said, "If you'd just answer five questions..."

"I'll answer one. But it'll cost you."

Her relief died a short death. "How much? I have a job, but it's barely enough to pay my tuition so I couldn't offer you anything significant—"

He looked so totally and utterly appalled, she knew she'd misunderstood. His expression said so, but in case she hadn't caught on, he leaned close, caging her in with one arm on the picnic table, the other on her shoulder, and said through his teeth, "You actually think I'd take money from you?"

Elizabeth tried leaning back, but she didn't have much room to maneuver, not without toppling over. "You...you said you don't have a job."

"Wrong." He looked ready to do that neck wringing she'd worried about. "I said I'm not employed here. For your information, Red, I more than pay my own way. Not that my financial situation is any business of yours."

"But..." It was one of the questions in her survey, though luckily this time she had the good sense to forfeit it. "Of course not. I didn't mean to suggest—"

"If you want me to answer a question, you'll have to loosen up. And before you start widening those big blue eyes at me again, I'm not suggestin' an illicit affair."

Her heart almost stopped, but for the life of her she wasn't entirely sure if it was relief or disappointment she felt. No one had ever offered her an illicit affair, and the idea held a certain amount of appeal. Not that she'd ever accept, of course, but still... "What, exactly, are you suggesting?"

"A swim. In the lake. Me and you."

The big green murky lake behind her? The lake he'd pulled that enormous fish out of—then thrown it back so it was still in there? The lake where any number of things could be living? Never mind that she didn't even own a bathing suit, the thought of getting into that lake positively terrified her. Hoping against hope, she said, "I don't understand."

"It's easy, Lizzy. I want you here tomorrow, same time, wearing a swimsuit instead of all that armor. And I want you to relax with me, to take a nice leisurely swim. Maybe if you loosen up a bit, I won't even mind so much answering a question for you."

To make certain she understood before she agreed to anything, she asked, "And in exchange, you'll answer my questions?"

"No, I'll answer one question. Just one. Any question you like. You can even make notes in that damn little book of yours." He eyed her mouth again, then shook his head. "And who knows, if all goes well, maybe we can work out another deal."

"For another question?"

He shrugged, looking reluctant but strangely resigned.

Elizabeth had the sneaking suspicion he was trying to bluff her, to force her to back out. But she was fascinated. Such unusual behavior for a hero! She could almost imagine the response she'd get from this thesis—if anyone even believed it. But there had to be some redeeming information there, something that would make her research all that more complete, valuable and applicable.

In the end, there was really only one decision she could make. She held out her hand, and after a moment, Gabe took it.

His hand was so large, so tanned. And he felt hot. She gulped, shored up her courage, and with a smile that almost hurt, she said, "Deal."

HE COULDN'T BELIEVE he was running late.

If anything, he'd planned to be on the dock, sunning himself, a man without a care, when she arrived. Truth was, he felt strangely anxious. He grinned at the novelty of it.

"You've been doing a lot of that this morning."

Gabe turned to his brother Sawyer. "What?"

"Smiling like a fool."

"Maybe I have good reason."

"And what would that be?"

"None of your business." Gabe, still grinning, finished running caulk around the windowpane then wiped his hands on a small towel. "That should do you, Sawyer. From now on, don't let kids play baseball in your office, hear?"

Honey hustled up to his side with a tall glass of iced tea. Bless her, he did like all the doting she felt compelled to do. Having a sister-in-law was a right nice thing. "Thanks, Honey."

"What are you so happy about, Gabe?"

Uh oh. He glanced at Sawyer, saw his smirk and concentrated on drinking his tea. Sawyer knew without a doubt that he wouldn't even consider telling Honey to mind her own business. By virtue of being female, she was due all the respect his brothers didn't warrant. He just naturally tempered himself around women—well, all but Red. She seemed to bring out the oddest reactions from him. Damned if he wasn't looking forward to seeing her again.

What would she look like in a bikini?

"There he goes, grinning again."

"Actually," Gabe said, ignoring his brother, "I was just thinking of a woman." That was true enough, and not at all uncommon. In fact, Honey gave him a fond look of indulgence, patted his shoulder, then went to her husband's side. Sawyer sure was a lucky cuss. Honey was a sexy little woman—not that he thought of her that way, her being in the family and all. But he wasn't blind. She was a real looker, and best of all, she loved his brother to distraction.

Sawyer gave a grievous sigh. "He's in lust again. Just look at him."

That drew Gabe up short. Lust? Hell, no, he didn't feel lust for Little Red. Amusement maybe, because she was unaccountably funny with her freckles and her red corkscrew curls that hung all the way down to her fanny.

And frustration, because she simply had no idea how to accept no for an answer and she trussed herself up in those schoolmarm clothes, to the point a guy couldn't even tell what he was seeing.

Maybe even annoyance, because her stubbornness rivaled his brother Morgan's, and that was saying a mouthful. But not lust.

He grunted, earning an odd look from Sawyer.

His invitation for a swim was simply his way of keeping the upper hand. And thinking that, he said to Sawyer, "If a funny little red-haired woman tries to talk to you about me, don't tell her a damn thing, okay?"

Sawyer and Honey blinked at him in confusion, but he didn't bother to explain. He hurried off. Knowing Red, if he was too late, she'd give up on him and go home. She wasn't the type of woman who'd wait around, letting a guy think she'd be happy to see him when he did show up. No, Red would probably get her back all stiff and go off asking questions of every available body in the area.

And he really didn't want anyone filling her head with that nonsense about heroes. Best that he talked to her himself. And that was another reason he'd engineered the date. No, take that back. Not a date. An appointment. Yeah, that sounded better. He'd arranged an appointment so that at least she'd get her stupid story straight.

Hell, he had plenty of reasons for seeing her again, and none of them were about lust.

He did wonder what she'd look like in a bikini, though.

SHE WAS STILL in full armor.

Gabe frowned as he climbed out of his car and

started down the hill. Judging by the color of that long braid hanging almost to the dock, the woman with her back to him was one Miss Elizabeth Parks. And she wasn't wearing a bikini. He consoled himself with the fact that at least she was waiting for him. There was a certain amount of masculine satisfaction in that.

The second he stepped on the dock, she turned her head. He noticed then that she was sitting cross-legged instead of dangling her feet in the water. She had her shoes and frilly little white socks on. Socks in this heat? He stopped and frowned at her. "Where's your swimsuit?"

She frowned right back. "I have it on under my dress. Surely you didn't think I'd drive here in it? And you're late."

She turned away and with her elbows on her knees, propped her chin on a fist and stared at the lake.

Gabe surveyed her stiff back and slowly approached. He wasn't quite sure what to expect of her, so he said carefully, "I'm glad you waited."

With a snort, she answered, "You made it a part of the deal. If I want to ask you one measly question, I had to be here." She waved a dismissive hand. "I figured you'd show up sooner or later."

Not exactly the response he'd hoped for. In fact, she'd taken all the fun out of finding her still here. "Well, skin out of those clothes then, so we can get in. It's hot enough to send a lizard running for shade. That water's going to feel good."

She didn't look at all convinced. Peering at him

with one eye scrunched against the sunshine and her small pointed nose wrinkled, she said, "The thing is, I'm not at all keen on doing that."

"What?"

"The swimsuit thing. I've never had much reason to swim, and this boat dock is pretty crowded...."

"You want privacy?" Now why did that idea intrigue him? But it was a good idea, not because he'd be alone with her. No, that had nothing to do with it. But that way, if she asked her dumb hero question, no one else would be around to contradict him.

He liked that idea. "We can take a fishing boat back to a cove. No one's there, at least, not close. There might be a few fishermen trolling by, or the occasional skier, but they won't get near enough to shore to look you over too good." He gave her a crooked grin. "Your modesty will be preserved." *Except from me.*

Her face colored. "It's not that I think I'd draw much attention, you understand. It's just not something I'm used to."

With the way she managed to cover herself from shins to throat, he didn't doubt it. "No problem. The cove is real peaceful. I swim there all the time. Come on." He reached down a hand for her, trying not to look as excited as he suddenly felt. "Do you know how to swim?"

She ignored his hand and lumbered to her feet, dusting off her bottom as she did so. "Not really."

Rather than let her get to him, he dropped his hand and pretended it didn't matter. But he couldn't recall ever having such a thing happen in his entire life, and he knew right then and there he didn't like it worth a damn. "Then you'll need a flotation belt. There's some in the boat. You got a towel?"

"My stuff is there." She pointed to the shore where a large colorful beach towel, a floppy brimmed hat and a pair of round, blue-lens sunglasses had been tossed. Next to the pile was her infamous notepad, which made him frown.

Gabe had his towel slung around his neck, his mirrored glasses already in place and his hat on backward. He carried a stocked cooler in his free hand. "Let's go."

He led her to a small metal fishing boat, then despite her efforts to step around him, helped her inside. The boat swayed, and she nearly lost her balance. She would have fallen overboard if he hadn't held on to her.

He managed not to smirk.

He tossed her stuff in to her, then said, "Take a seat up front and put on a belt. If you fall in, it'll keep you from drowning until I can fish you out."

"Like you did the carp?"

Her teasing smile made his stomach tighten. "Naw, I kissed the fish and threw him back in for luck." He glanced at her, then added, "I wouldn't do that to you."

Her owl-eyed expression showed her confusion. Let her wonder if he meant he wouldn't kiss her or he wouldn't throw her back. Maybe keeping her guessing would take some of the edge off her cockiness. He hid his satisfaction as he stepped into the boat and tilted the motor into the water. He braced his feet apart, gave the rip cord a tug, and the small trolling motor hummed to life.

After seating himself comfortably, he said, "We won't break any speed records, but the ride'll be smooth."

"Is this your boat?"

"Naw. Belongs to Rosemary. But she lets me use it whenever I want."

"Because you do work around the dock for her?"

Tendrils of hair escaped her long thick braid and whipped into her face. She held them back with one hand while she watched him. The dress she wore was made like a tent—no shape at all. From what he could see, it pulled on over her head, without a button or zipper or tie anywhere to be found. The neck was rounded and edged with lace, and the sleeves were barely there. But at least it was a softer material, something kind of like a T-shirt, and a pale yellow that complemented her red hair and bright blue eyes.

Gabe pulled himself away from that distraction and reminded himself that lust had nothing to do with his motivation today. He smiled at her. "Is that your question?"

"What?"

"Your one allotted question. You want to know about me working at the boat dock?"

Her frown was fierce. "Just making conversation."

"Uh-huh. You know what I think? I think you figured you'd sneak a whole bunch of questions in on me and I wouldn't notice."

She bit her lips and looked away. Gabe couldn't help but laugh out loud, it was so obvious she'd been caught. Damn, but she was a surprise. She sat there with her little feet pressed primly together—those damn lacy ankle socks somehow looking kind of sexy all of a sudden—while her snowy white sneakers got damp with the water in the bottom of the boat. Her hands were clasped together in her lap, holding onto her big floppy hat, her eyes squinted against the wind and sun. Her freckles were even more noticeable out here on the lake. She wasn't exactly what you'd call a pretty woman, certainly not a bombshell like Sawyer's Honey or Morgan's Misty. But there was definitely something about her....

"Where are we going?"

She sat facing him in the boat, so he pointed behind her to where the land stretched out and the only living things in sight were a few cows grazing along the shoreline. The man-made lake was long and narrow, shaped a lot like a river with vacation cabins squeezed into tight rows along both sides. Several little fingers of water stretched out to form small coves here and there, only a few of which were still owned by farmers and hadn't been taken over by developers. The land Gabe lived on with his brothers had a cove like that, a narrow extension of the main lake, almost entirely cut off from the boating traffic since it was so shallow. But it made for great swimming and fishing, which was what the brothers used it for.

Though they didn't have any cows there, it was peaceful and natural and they loved it, refusing to sell no matter how many times they were asked and regardless of the offer. They jointly owned a lot of property, and in two spots runoff from the main lake had formed a smaller lake and a pond. Gabe intended to build a house on that site some day.

"We're going *there?*" Lizzy asked, interrupting his thoughts. She sounded horrified.

Gabe bobbed an eyebrow. "It's real private."

"Are the cows friendly?"

"Most bovines are. You just don't want to walk behind them."

"They kick?"

She sounded appalled again, so he had to really struggle to keep from laughing. "Nope. But you have to be real careful where you step."

"Oh."

Slowing the motor, Gabe let the boat glide forward until they'd rounded the cove and nudged as far inside as possible. Someone in years past had installed a floating dock, but it had definitely seen better days. It tended to list to one side, with three corners out of the water and one corner under, covered by moss. But at least it was a good six feet square and didn't sink if you climbed on it.

Gabe threw a rope around a metal cleat on the side of the dock. It was strange, but his heart was already pounding like mad—he had no idea why—and he had to force himself to speak calmly.

He looked at her, saw her shy, averted gaze and felt the wild thrum of excitement. He swallowed hard. "This is as far as we get, so you can skin out of that dress now."

She peeked at him, then away. "Why don't you go ahead and get in, then I'll...inch my way in?"

"Have you ever driven a boat?"

"No."

"Do you know how to start it?"

She glanced dubiously at the pull start for the motor, then shook her head. "I don't think so."

He nodded. "So at least I know you're not plotting on getting me overboard then taking off."

Her eyes widened. "I wouldn't do that." She chewed her lip, looking undecided, then admitted, "It's just that I hadn't figured on how to go about stripping off my clothes out here in the open."

"With me and the cows watching?"

"Right."

He could have offered a few suggestions, but that would be crass. Besides, he was afraid his suggestions would offend her. Likely they would.

Oh, hell, he knew damn good and well they would.

"All right. I'll turn my back. But don't take too long. You can put your folded things on the cooler so they won't get wet." Before he could change his mind, he turned his back, stepped on a seat and dove in. He heard her squeal as the small boat rocked wildly.

The water was shallow, so he made the dive straight out, and seconds later his head broke the water. He could easily stand, so he waded to the dock, keeping his head averted, then rested his folded arms over the edge of the aged wood. He could hear her undressing.

"The water feels great." His voice shook, damn it.

"It's...green."

He cleared his throat. "Because of the moss." She probably had her shoes off already, and those ridiculous, frilly, feminine little socks that looked like they'd come from a fetish catalogue, though he doubted she knew it. He pictured her wearing those socks—and nothing else. The picture was vague because he had no idea what the hell her body looked like, but the thought still excited him. Dumb.

Did she only have on the dress, or was she wearing other stuff over her suit? He cleared his throat and mustered his control. "Aren't you done yet?"

"Well...yeah."

His head snapped around, and he stared. She stood there, pale slender arms folded over her middle, long legs pressed together, shoulders squared as if in challenge. And her suit wasn't a bikini, not that it mattered one little bit.

"Damn, woman." The words were a choked whisper, hot and touched with awe. It felt like his eyes bugged out of his head.

She shifted nervously, uncrossing and recrossing her arms, taking her weight from one foot to the other, making the supple muscles in her calves and thighs move seductively.

Gabe had no idea if she blushed or not because he couldn't get his gaze off her body and onto her face.

The one-piece suit was simple, a pale lime green, and it covered enough skin to make a grandma happy. But what it left uncovered...

Her plump breasts made his mouth water with the instinct of Pavlov's dog. High, round...he wondered for a single heartbeat if they were real or enhanced. He stared, hard, unaware of her discomfort, her uncertainty. Nothing in the suit suggested it capable of that incredible support. There were no underwires, no lined bra cups. The suit was a sleek, simple design, and it hugged her like her own skin.

The visible outline of soft nipples drew him, making his imagination go wild. He wanted to see them tight and puckered, straining for his mouth.

Breathing deeply, he traced her body with his gaze, to the shaping of her rib cage, the indention of a navel, the rounded slope of her mound.

Heat rolled through him, making his nostrils flare. He could easily picture her naked, and did so, tormenting himself further.

Surely even the cows were agog. She had the most symmetrically perfect feminine body he'd ever seen, and the lake water no longer felt so cool. His groin grew thick and heavy, hot. It was unexpected, this instantaneous reaction he had to her. Women didn't affect him this way. He'd learned control early on and hadn't had an unwanted erection since his teens. He chose when to be involved; he did not get sucked into a vortex of lust!

But there was no denying what he felt at this moment. It annoyed him, with himself, not her. She did nothing to entice him, other than to stand there and let him look his fill.

Just as he'd suspected, her freckles decorated other parts of her body, not just her face. Her shoulders were lightly sprinkled with them—and her thighs. His heartbeat lost its even rhythm. Damn. He hadn't known freckles could be so incredibly sexy.

One thing was certain, he was sure glad he'd

brought her here so that every guy on the lake wasn't able to gawk at her.

Hell, he was doing enough gawking for all of them.

Pulling himself together, he cleared his throat again and looked at her face. Her head was down, her long braid hanging over a shoulder, touching a hipbone. He bit his lip, feeling the heavy thumping of his heart, the tautness of his muscles. "Lizzy?"

Her arms tightened around herself. "Hmm?"

Belatedly he understood her anxiety at being on display. He felt like a jerk, and tried for a teasing tone despite the urgency hammering through him. "You comin' in or not?"

"Do I get a choice?"

He didn't hesitate. "No."

Slowly her gaze lifted to his. "You'd better be worth this."

Oh, he'd show her just how worthwhile he could— No, wait. Wrong thought. He hadn't brought her here for that. He'd brought her here to convince her to forget about her silly ideas of heroism.

He scowled with determination, but his carnal thoughts seemed less and less wrong with every second she stood there, her small body the epitome of sexual temptation. He unglued his tongue and said, "Come on. Quit stalling."

She licked her lips and he groaned, practically feeling the stroke of her small pink tongue.

She glared at him suspiciously, then looked over the side of the boat, looked at him and licked her lips again. "How?"

Without even thinking about it, he found himself

wading to the boat, holding up his arms and inviting her into them.

And just like that, she closed her eyes, muttered a quiet prayer and fell in against him.

3

GABE FOUND his arms filled with warm, soft woman. It wasn't the first time, of course, but it sure felt different from any other time. Unexpectedly, her scent surrounded him. Lizzy smelled sweet, with a unique hint of musk that pulled at him. Her fingers were tight in his hair, her arms wrapped around his head in a death grip. His mind went almost blank. He could feel her firm, rounded bottom against his right forearm where he'd instinctively hooked her closer, to keep her from falling when she'd jumped in against him. His left arm was around her narrow waist, his large hand splayed wide so that his fingers spanned her back.

More momentous than that, though, was the fact that his face was pressed between her breasts. They certainly felt real enough. Jolted by the sexual press of her body, he froze, not even breathing. She was wrapped around him like a vine, but she didn't seem to notice the intimacy of their position.

Gabe noticed. Damn, but he noticed.

He shifted the tiniest bit so that his hand could cuddle a full, round cheek, and felt the shock of the touch all the way to his throbbing groin. She panted, but not with excitement.

"Lizzy?" His voice was muffled, thanks to having

his face buried in lush breasts. His hand on her bottom continued to caress her, almost with a will of its own.

Her arms tightened, her legs shifting to move around his hips in a jerky, desperate attempt to get closer to him. The movement brought the open, hot juncture of her thighs against his abdomen, and he sucked in a startled, strangled breath. If they were naked, if he slipped her down just a few inches, he could be inside her.

He was losing his grip on propriety real fast.

"Lizzy," he said, speaking low to keep from jarring her, "you're afraid of the water?"

Her growled, "No...*yes*," almost made him smile. Even now, she tried to hide behind her prickly pride.

"It's okay. There's nothing in here to bother you." Nothing but him, only she didn't need to know that.

"I've never...never swam in a lake before."

Her lips were right above his ear. She sounded breathless, and her voice trembled. "There's nothing to be afraid of," he crooned, and then, because he couldn't help himself, he turned his face slightly and nuzzled his nose against the plump, firm curve of her breast.

She screamed, making his ears ring. In the next instant, she launched herself out of his arms and thrashed her way wildly to the floating dock. The back view of her awkward, hasty climb from the water didn't do a thing to cool his libido. She seemed to be all long legs and woman softness and enticing freckles. The suit, now wet, was even more revealing. Not more revealing than a bikini, but that didn't seem to matter to his heated libido. He watched her huddle on the dock, wrapping her arms around herself, then hurriedly survey the water.

He owed her an apology. That made him disgruntled enough to grouse, "I'll be deaf for an hour. You screech like a wet hen."

Lizzy shook her head, and her teeth chattered. "Something touched me. Something brushed against my leg!"

Gabe stalled. So she hadn't screamed over his forwardness? From the looks of her, he thought, seeing how wild-eyed she appeared, she probably hadn't even noticed that he was turned on, that he'd been attempting to kiss her breast. Making a small sound of exasperation, Gabe said, "It was probably just a fish."

She shuddered in visible horror. "What kind of fish?"

He looked around, peering through the water, which was stirred up from her churning retreat. "There." Pointing, he indicated a small silvery fish pecking at bubbles on the surface of the lake.

Lizzy carefully leaned forward on her hands and knees, making her breasts sway beneath the wet green suit. "Is it a baby?"

He kept his gaze glued to her body. His tongue felt thick and his jaw tight. "No. A bluegill. They don't get much bigger than that."

Her gaze lifted and met his, forcing him to stop staring at her body. "What'd you expect," he asked, "Jaws?"

Her face heated. To Gabe, she looked sexy and enticing and adorable, perched on the edge of the floating dock, her bottom in the air, her eyes wide and her cheeks rosy. Her brows angled. "Are you laughing at me?"

"Nope." He waded over to her then leaned on his forearms. No way could he join her on the dock. His wet cutoffs wouldn't do much to hide his erection. "I didn't realize you were afraid of the water," he told her gently. "You should have said something."

After a deep breath, she sat back. She drew her knees up and wrapped her arms around them. "I was embarrassed," she admitted with a sideways look at him. "I hate being cowardly."

"It's not cowardly to be unsure of things you're not familiar with."

"Will you still answer my question?"

Annoyed that she wouldn't forget her purpose for even a minute, he shrugged. "Get it over with."

Her blue eyes lit with excitement, and she dropped her arms to lean toward him. Her nipples, he couldn't help noticing, were long and pointed.

She smiled. "What were you thinking when you went into the water to save those kids?"

"Thinking?"

"Yes. You saw they were in trouble, and you wanted to help. What did you think about? How you'd get them out, the danger, that your own life wasn't important..."

"Oh, for pity's sake. It wasn't anything like that." Forgetting that he needed to stay in the water, he levered himself up beside her on the dock in one fluid movement. The dock bobbed, making her gasp and flatten her hands on the wood for balance. Water sluiced off his body as he dropped next to her then shook his head like a wet dog. Lizzy made a grab for him to keep from getting knocked in, but she released him just as quickly and frowned at him.

"So what was it like?"

He leaned back on his elbows and surveyed the bright sun, the cloudless sky. "Hell, I don't know. I didn't think anything. I saw the boat, saw the kids—and just reacted." Before she could say anything about that, he added, "Anyone would have done the same."

"No one did do the same. Only you."

He shrugged. "I'd already gone in. There was no reason for anyone else to."

"You were quicker to react."

"Maybe I just noticed the problem first."

When she shifted to face him, Gabe again eyed her breasts. He felt obsessed. Would her nipples be pink or a rosy brown?

She touched his arm. "Were you afraid?"

Annoyed by her persistence, he leaned back on the dock, covering his eyes with a forearm. "That's another question." Gabe wondered if she even realized he was male. He had a raging hard-on, he'd been staring at her breasts with enough intensity to set her little red head on fire, and she hadn't even noticed. He snorted. Or maybe she just didn't care. Maybe she found him so lacking, so unappealing, he could be naked and it wouldn't affect her.

Her small hand smacked against his shoulder. "Not fair! You didn't even really answer the first question."

He lowered his arm enough to glare at her. "You didn't really swim, so we're even."

Mulish determination set her features, then she turned to the water. Distaste and fear stiffened her shoulders and, amazed, Gabe realized she was going to get in.

"Lizzy..." He reached for her shoulder.

"If a snake eats me, it'll be on your head!" She stuck a toe in the water.

Smiling, Gabe pulled her back. "All right. I'll answer your question."

The tension seemed to melt right out of her. "You will?"

He sighed long and loud to let her know she was a pest. *Yeah, right.* "It beats seeing that look of terror on your face." He flicked her nose as he said it, to let her know he was teasing.

She paid him no mind, speaking to herself in a mumble. "I wish I had my notebook."

Gabe came to his knees, caught the line holding the boat secure and pulled it in. It was a stretch, but he was able to reach her bag and hand it to her. "There you go."

Her smile was beatific. "Thank you."

He gave her a gentlemanly nod. She didn't notice his body, but at least she appreciated his manners. "No problem. Not that I can tell you anything interesting enough to write down."

The look of concentration on her face as she pulled out her notepad told him she disagreed. Gabe thought now cute she was when she went all serious and sincere.

Not that a cute, redheaded virago should have interested him. Beyond making him unaccountably hot, that was.

Nose wrinkled against the glare of the sun, she looked at him and said, "I'm ready."

She looked ready, he thought, unable to keep his mind focused on the fact that he wasn't interested. Posed on the dock as she was, she made a fetching picture. Her long legs were folded to the side in the primmest manner possible, given her body was more bare than not. She tilted her head and pursed her lips in serious cogitation. The bright sunshine glinted off her hair, showing different colored strands of gold and amber and bronze. Midway down, her braid was darker from being wet, and it rested, heavy and thick, along her side. Her skin shone with a fine mist of sweat, intensifying her sweet scent so that with every small breeze he breathed her in.

His skin felt too hot, but not because of the sun.

Gabe wondered what she'd do if he eased her backward and covered her with his body. Would she scream again? He groaned, causing her to lift one brow. She hadn't screamed last time because of him. No, she hadn't even noticed his attention.

"What's wrong?"

Other than the fact he was attracted to a woman who shouldn't have appealed to him and didn't return the favor? He groaned again. "Not a thing." Once again he reclined on the small dock, crossing his arms behind his head. He was too long for the thing, so he let his knees stick over the side and hung his feet in the water. "Let's see. What did I think? Well, I cursed. I know that."

Pencil to paper, she asked, "What did you say?"

"It's not something to be repeated in front of a lady."

"Oh. I understand."

She scribbled quickly across her paper, making Gabe curious. But he already knew she wasn't about to reveal her words to him. "Thing is," he admitted, "I don't really remember thinking anything. I saw the kids and the woman, saw the boat, and I just dove in. I knew they could get hurt, and I knew I could help." He shrugged, not looking at her. "It's no more complicated than that."

"So," she said, her eyes narrowed in thoughtful speculation, "your heroism was instinctive, like a basic part of you?"

"It wasn't heroism, damn it, but yeah, I guess it was instinctive to just dive in and do what I could."

"Did you even think about the danger to yourself?"

Here he was, Gabe thought, lounging in front of her, half naked, and she hadn't even looked at him once. He knew, because he'd been watching her, waiting to see what she'd do when she saw he was aroused. She'd barely noticed him at all except to give him her disapproving looks.

It nettled him that she was on this ridiculous hero kick. He was a man, same as any other, but that obviously didn't interest her at all. He wanted her interest, though he shouldn't have. But looking at her made him forget that she wasn't his type, that he didn't care what she thought, that he was only here today on a lark, as a way to pass the time and have some fun.

He wasn't used to a woman being totally oblivious to his masculinity, and he damn sure didn't like it.

He wouldn't, in fact, tolerate it.

Speaking in a low, deliberately casual tone, he reminded her, "That's another question. I told you I'd answer one."

"But..."

"We could make another deal." He closed his eyes as he said it, as if it didn't matter to him one way or the other. The ensuing silence was palpable. He felt the dock rock the tiniest bit and knew she was shifting. In nervousness? In annoyance? If he looked at her, he'd be able to read the emotions in her big blue eyes. But he didn't want to see if it was only frustration that lit her gaze. He waited, held his breath.

And finally she said, "All right. What deal?"

He opened his eyes and pinned her, his heart pumping hard, his muscles twitching. "I'll answer another question—for a kiss."

She blinked at him, her long, gold-tipped lashes lazily drifting down and up again, as if she couldn't quite believe what he'd said. "A kiss?"

"Mm." He pointed to his mouth. His gaze never left her face, watching her closely. Anticipation, thick and electric, hummed in his veins. "Right here, right now. One question, one kiss."

She shifted again. The lake was still, the only sounds those of a cow occasionally bawling or the soft splash of a frog close to shore. Lizzy nibbled her lips—lush, wet lips. Her gaze, bright and direct, never left his face. She drew a deep breath that made her breasts strain against the clinging material of the suit.

Her blue eyes darkened and her words, soft and uncertain, made him jerk in response.

"What..." she whispered, her breath catching before she cleared her throat and started again. "What if I kiss you twice?"

AT LEAST he was smooth-shaven today, Elizabeth thought as she watched Gabe's face, saw his eyes glitter and grow intent. She felt tense from her toes to her eyebrows, struggling endlessly to keep her gaze on his face and off his lean, muscled body. He was by far the most appealing man she'd ever known—and the most maddening.

When he continued to watch her, his eyes heavier, the blue so hot they looked electric, she made a sound of impatience. "Well?"

In husky tones, he asked, "Two kisses, hm?"

Much more and she'd be racing for the shore. She couldn't take his intensity, the way he stared at her, stroked her with his gaze. Her breasts felt full, her belly sweetly pulled with some indefinable ache. What could he possibly hope to gain with his present attitude? She didn't for a minute think he was actually attracted to her. For one thing, men simply didn't pay that much attention to her. More often than not, she could be invisible for all the notice they took. Secondly, she still remembered his reaction when they'd met. Gabriel Kasper had found her amusing, annoying and, judging by the way he'd looked her over, totally unappealing.

Perhaps, she continued to reason, he only hoped to intimidate her! That would certainly make sense. She swallowed hard and refused to back down. She needed his knowledge. She craved the information that would make her understand what special qualities created a hero. Or a heroine.

His mouth, firm and sensual, wholly masculine, twitched slightly. "Two kisses, two questions."

It was what she'd wanted. And then he added, "Ten kisses, ten questions—but understand, Lizzy, I'm only a man. Kisses are all I can barter and remain a...gentleman." He turned his head slightly toward her, and his voice dropped. "Or does that matter?"

She stiffened. Did he suggest her kisses could make him lose control? Not likely! Mustering her courage, she asked, "Why are you doing this?"

"This...what?"

She waved a hand at his lazy form. "This game. Why trade for kisses? Why trade at all? Is it really so hard to answer a short interview?"

His jaw tightened, and he shut his eyes again. After a moment, still looking more asleep than alert, he said, "You need to loosen up a little, Red. It's a nice afternoon, the sun is warm, the water's cool. We're all alone. Why not play a little?" He looked at her, his gaze probing. "Is the idea of kissing me so repulsive?"

She filled her lungs with a deep breath. So she was just a game, a way to pass the time. The arrogant jerk. She'd have to remember to make a note of that, that some heroes were not always perfect in their behavior, some of them enjoyed toying with women.

She straightened her shoulders, refusing to let him intimidate her. "No, not at all."

"Then we don't have a problem, do we?"

The only problem, evidently, was her inhibition. But in the face of all she could learn from him, did her reserve really matter? Suddenly determined, she squelched her nervousness and said with firm resolve, "Okay, a kiss for a question."

She waited, braced for his sensual assault, but Gabe simply continued to watch her. Not by so much as the flick of an eyelash did he move. Her stomach cramped the tiniest bit and she lifted an eyebrow.

She was both disappointed and relieved when she asked, "You've changed your mind?"

With one indolent shake of his head, Gabe crooked a finger at her. "C'mere, Red. You're going to do the kissing, not me."

In reaction to his potent look, more than her stomach cramped, but the feeling wasn't at all unpleasant.

"Oh." She looked at his gorgeous body stretched out in front of her—and started shaking. His shoulders were wide and bunched with muscles, as were his biceps. The undersides of his arms were smooth, slightly lighter than the rest of his skin. She'd never considered a man's armpits sexy before—just the thought was ludicrous—but she'd never seen Gabriel Kasper's. Seeing the hair under his arms was somehow too intimate, like a private showing. She looked away from that part of him.

His chest, tanned and sprinkled with golden

brown hair, had the lean hard contours that spoke of a natural athlete. Her pulse fluttered.

His abdomen was flat, sculpted, and if his underarms were too personal, his navel was downright sexual. The way his body hair swirled around it, then became a silky line that disappeared into the very low waistband of his shorts... Her eyes widened.

With his wet cutoffs clinging to his body, there was no way to miss his obvious arousal. Fascinated, she couldn't help but stare for a moment. Never, not in real life, anyway, had she seen an erection. Heat exploded inside her, making her cheeks pulse, her vision blur.

Her gaze flew to his face, desperate, confused, *excited*. His grin, slow and wicked, taunted her. He didn't say a word, and she knew he was waiting for her to back down.

She couldn't. Not now, not with him challenging her. But...

Licking her lips, Elizabeth croaked, "Are you sure we should do this?"

He shrugged one hard shoulder in a show of negligence. "No one will see. Don't be a coward, Lizzy. It's just a kiss."

Just a kiss. She remembered how those women on the dock had hung on him, how every woman who passed in a boat had stared at him with hunger. He was used to kissing, used to so much more. She couldn't recall any other man in all her acquaintance ever demanding such a thing from her. No wonder she was at a loss as to how to proceed. She preferred to arm herself with knowledge, to learn from a book what she didn't understand. But she hadn't known to research this particular theme. She frowned with that thought. Were there books to help you bone up on kissing a sexy-as-sin, half-dressed reclining man?

She eyed him warily. "Why don't you...sit up?" The idea of leaning over him, of being that close to so much masculine flesh, flustered her horribly.

Without hesitation, Gabe shook his head. "Naw, I'm already comfortable. So quit stalling."

He was right; the quicker she got it over with, the better. Like getting a tooth pulled, it meant just a flinch of pain, and then you were done.

Not giving herself time to think about it, she slapped one hand flat on the dock beside his head, bent down and brushed her mouth over his in a flash of movement. She straightened just as quickly and, avoiding his gaze, put her pencil to paper. Her voice shook slightly, but she ignored the tremor as she asked, "Now, when you leaped into the water with the runaway boat, were you afraid?"

"No."

She waited, her pencil ready, but he said no more. Elizabeth rounded on him, her nerves too frazzled for more games. "That's an awfully simplified answer."

He gave her a wry look. "It was an awfully simplified kiss."

Unable to help herself, she looked at his mouth. Her lips still tingled from the brief contact with his. It took all her concentration not to lick her lips, not to chew on them. Her heartbeat was still racing too quickly, her stomach was in knots of anticipation...no! Dread, not anticipation. She had to be philosophical. "You mean, if I made the kiss longer..."

So softly she could barely hear him, he said, "Why don't you give it a try and see?"

She could do this! She was not a fainthearted ninny. Determination stiffened her spine. Sensual awareness sharpened her senses. She gave one quick nod.

Laying the pencil and paper aside, she bent, clasped her palms over his ears to anchor both him and herself, then kissed him for all she was worth.

Never having done much kissing, she had no idea if she was doing it right. But she mashed her mouth tightly to his, turned her head subtly so their lips meshed, and sighed. Or maybe it was more a growl filled with resolution.

His lips felt firm, warm. This close, his scent was stronger, drifting over her, making her insides fill with a new and unexpected need. He was so hot, his skin where they touched almost burning her. Her chin bumped his, their noses rubbed together, and her wrists rested on his silky hot shoulders. She stopped moving her mouth and simply breathed deeply.

Gabe groaned, then promptly laughed, startling her enough that she sat up and stared at him in hurt and confusion.

With a small smile, using only one rough finger, he stroked her bottom lip. His words were as gentle as his touch, and just as devastating. "You haven't done much kissing, have you, Lizzy?"

Indignation would be misplaced; obviously, he

could already tell she was inexperienced, so why should she deny it or be embarrassed? He could see what she looked like, had even used the same insulting taunt of Red she'd heard in grade school. He could probably guess at the other names—freckle face and scarecrow. And no doubt he understood the way she'd been ignored in high school, when all the boys were chasing cheerleaders with bubbly personalities and model faces.

None of that hurt her anymore. She had found more important things to do with her time. With an accepting shrug, she agreed. "Pitifully little, actually." And even that was an exaggeration.

Amazingly, his smile turned seductive. He came up on his right elbow, wrapped the fingers of his left hand around her nape and pulled her close. Against her mouth, he whispered, "Then allow me."

His tongue... Oh gracious. His mouth opened hers with almost no effort. His tongue touched, teased, not really entering her mouth, but making her crazed with small licks and tastes, softly, wetly stroking. She held herself very still so as not to disturb him or interrupt his progress.

Slowly, in infinitesimal degrees, he pulled his mouth away. His hand still held her neck, his fingers caressing, and he stared at her mouth. "You're not kissing me back, Lizzy."

"I..." She hadn't realized he wanted her to. All her senses had been attuned to what he was doing, not what she might do. "Sorry."

With a groan, he took her mouth again, not so gently this time, a hungry greed coming through to curl her toes and make her fingers go numb. Elizabeth leaned into him, tilted her head the tiniest bit to better accept his mouth. She braced her hands against his chest, then jerked at how hot his skin was, the way his chest hair felt on her palms. Her breasts tingled, and below her stomach an insistent tingling demanded her attention.

She panted, and this time when his tongue touched her mouth, she captured it, stroking her tongue against him.

She wasn't sure if it was her heartbeat or his that rocked her. His hand left her head and captured her elbow. She found herself being slowly lowered to the dock, but she didn't care; she just wanted him to go on kissing her like this, creating the overwhelming turmoil inside her. She liked it. She liked him—his taste, his hardness, his scent.

His chest crushed her breasts, but not uncomfortably. It helped to ease the ache there, but then the ache intensified, especially when he moved, abrading her taut nipples. She gasped.

He was braced over her with his elbows on either side of her head. Tentatively, uncertain how far she should go, Elizabeth placed her hands on his back. His tongue stroked deeply and she moaned, arching into him.

Gabe pulled away with a curse. He stared into her eyes, his face so close she could see his individual lashes, and then with another soft curse he sat up and gave her his back.

She struggled for breath, not certain what had happened, if she'd done something wrong. She pressed her palms flat on the rough wooden dock and tried to secure herself. Her head was spinning, her heart beating so wildly she thought it might punch right out of her chest. Her lungs felt constricted, and she couldn't get enough air, which forced her to pant. And there was the most delicious tingling sensation deep inside her.

Gabe ran a hand though his hair, but he kept his back to her. She could see the straight line of his spine, the shift of his muscles as he, too, breathed deeply, quickly. With his attention elsewhere, she devoured him with her eyes. His skin was bronzed, testimony to how much time he spent on the lake, and a striking contrast to his fair hair and burning blue eyes. His damp shorts rode low on trim hips, but all she could see was tanned flesh.

Abruptly he shifted and speared her with a look, as if he'd sensed her regard. Over his shoulder, his eyes razor sharp, he growled, "Ask your damn question."

Still gasping, Elizabeth tried to gather her wits. Question? Her muddled mind came up with one reply. "Are you tanned all over?"

No sooner had the words left her mouth than she realized her mistake. Gabe's eyes widened comically. There was a moment of startled hesitation, then he threw his head back and laughed, the sound bouncing off the placid surface of the lake to return to her again and again, making her brain hurt and her face throb with heat.

Appalled, she started to sit up, but just that quick, Gabe caught her shoulders and pinned her in place.

"Where are you going?" he asked, his voice a

husky rumble. His mouth was still slightly curled in amusement.

Elizabeth tried to think. "I...I meant to ask you—"

"I know what you meant," he growled around another smile. "You want me to skin off my shorts so you can get a good look at my backside, just to appease your curiosity?"

Yes. "No, of course not!" He loomed over her, making rational thought impossible. But then, everything about Gabriel Kasper, from their first meeting to now, had been impossible.

"Liar." There was no insult in the accusation. In fact, he said it with amused affection, like an endearment. Then he kissed her again, softly, slowly. Elizabeth felt a constriction in her chest that had nothing to do with the way he held her and everything to do with the realization of all she'd missed in life.

The kiss wasn't consuming, but sweetly sensual. As Gabe lifted his head, he looked at her breasts, gently crushed against the hard planes of his chest. A slight tremble went through him as he swept one fingertip over the upper swell of each breast. "Are these real, sweetheart?"

Her breath strangled at the feel of his hot, rough finger stroking her there, in a place no man had ever touched. Eyes wide, she muttered, "What are you talking about?"

"You have such a sexy body." That taunting fingertip dipped slightly into her cleavage, causing her heart to pick up a quick, almost frantic beat. "And these breasts...so plump when you're so trim everywhere else. So soft when you're mostly firm. I just wondered if Mother Nature had really been so generous, or if you'd had a little help."

She stared at him, her mind blank, unable to think while he was touching her. She was aware of the sun hot against her skin, of the slight breeze that stirred the humid air, of the gentle lapping of the lake on the shore. But all of it was overshadowed by Gabe and the blue flare of his eyes.

Grinning, Gabe murmured, "Maybe I should just find out on my own?" His fingers spread over her chest, just below her collarbone, and jolted her into awareness.

She caught his wrist and stared at him hard. "They're real!" Then, because she was embarrassed over his attention, she muttered, "What a stupid question."

Gabe easily freed his hand from hers and wrapped his fingers around her skull, stroking her hair, smoothing it. "You must have never gone braless in your life."

Heat washed over her face, then down to her breasts. "Of course I haven't."

His thumb rubbed her cheekbone, the corner of her mouth. He shifted, his chest moving over hers, pressing. "Such a little innocent. Such a surprise." He looked at her mouth.

"Gabe?"

"Just one more," he whispered, husky and deep.

She thought to tell him that he'd owe her a lot of conversation for this, that she had plenty of questions he was going to have to answer, but the moment he took the kiss, she forgot all that.

His hand slid down her side to her waist, shaping her, measuring her, it seemed, then drifted to her hip. His touch was sure, his fingers rough, callused. He met bare skin on her upper thigh and made a raw sound of pleasure, causing her to quiver in response.

"So soft," he growled, his mouth against her throat, leaving damp kisses, sucking softly. Overwhelmed, alive, she tipped her head back to make it easier for him. His grip on her thigh tightened, and with little direction from him, she bent her knee and lifted one leg alongside his. The position neatly settled him into the cradle of her hips. She vaguely wondered why she didn't feel crushed, because he was so big, so hard.

He pushed, nestling closer, and his erection rubbed her in the most intimate spot imaginable. She gasped; he groaned.

She'd never felt a man on top of her before. The sensation was...*wonderful*. Scorching, enveloping, gratifying and at the same time stirring new needs.

Gabe dipped the tip of his tongue into her ear. That sensation, too, was astounding. How could such a simple act be so incredibly erotic? She heard his harsh breathing, felt his hot, moist breath and the hammering of his heart. He licked her ear. Stunned for just a moment, she froze, trying to take it all in.

He kissed her again. His mouth ate at hers, his teeth nipping, his tongue stroking. She melted, no longer capable of rational thought, simply reacting to what he did and how he did it.

In the next instant he was gone, sitting up beside her.

Elizabeth blinked in shock, uncertain what had happened or why he had pulled away so abruptly. She lay there, her eyes open but unseeing, trying to assimilate her senses. Gabe never hesitated. He caught her arms just above her elbows and jerked her upright so that she, too, was sitting, although not quite as steadily as he. It took a lot of effort not to flop down. She felt boneless and flushed and limp. Mute, she stared at him.

He gave her a grim, somewhat apologetic look and then she heard the motor. They both turned to stare at the entrance to the lake.

Seconds later a small fishing boat similar to the one they had used rounded the bend into the cove. Two older men, goofy hats hooked with a variety of lures perched on their heads, concentrated on the long fishing lines they had dragging in the water. Their voices were barely audible over the steady drone of the trolling motor.

They looked up in surprise when they noticed Gabe. Almost as one, their gazes turned to Elizabeth, and she felt herself turning pink with embarrassment. Good grief, could they tell what she and Gabe had been doing? Would they be able to look at her face and see it all?

Gabe moved, leaning forward to block her from view. He waved at the men, who waved back and continued to stare at them until their boat nearly went aground. With a disgruntled curse, the man in the back redirected their course and they puttered out of sight.

Gabe turned to her. His eyes were probing and direct. Unable to look away, Elizabeth thought how unfair it was that he could completely snare her with just a look. Eyes so light and clear a blue should have appeared cool, not fiery and passionate.

His fair hair shimmered beneath the sunshine, mussed from his swim—and from her fingers. Every muscle in his tensed body was delineated, drawing her eyes. He watched her so intently, she almost flinched.

Swallowing hard, Elizabeth tried to think of what to say. It was nearly impossible to muster a straight, businesslike face after that...that... She didn't know what to call it. It was certainly far more than a mere kiss. Admittedly, she lacked experience, but she was certainly not stupid. She knew the difference between kissing and what they'd just done.

It wasn't easy, but she reminded herself of her original purpose, her continued purpose. All her life she'd struggled to deal with the idiosyncrasies of heroism, why some had those qualities and some did not. Having heroism gave you the ability to change lives, lacking it could leave you forever empty.

She met Gabe's eyes and cleared her throat. "Well, after that, I expect an entire explanation for my thesis."

She hadn't meant to sound so cold and detached; what she really felt was far different from those simple emotions. She'd only meant to stress the point of what they were doing and why.

Gabe's eyes darkened, narrowed, the heat leaving them as if it had never been there. His jaw flexed once, then stilled. He stared at her mouth and said, "You'll get it."

4

HE WANTED to shake her, to... God, he'd never had the inclination to do any more than make love with a woman, laugh with her, tease. But Lizzy had him crazed.

He'd all but taken her on the damn dock, out in the open, on the lake, for crying out loud.

And she'd have let him.

He sensed it in his bones. He knew women, knew how they thought, what they felt, when they were turned on and how to turn them on. Little Red had been wild. She'd bit his bottom lip, sucked on his tongue, lifted her hips into the thrust of his... She'd strained against him, trying to get closer, and her fluttering heartbeat had let him measure each new degree of her excitement. She'd been on the ragged edge. He could have slipped his fingers past the leg band of her suit and stroked her over the edge with very little effort.

But now she watched him as though it had never happened, demanding answers to questions that were beyond stupid.

"I need to cool off." With no more warning than that, Gabe went over the side of the dock. He swam down until he touched the bottom, feeling around for a shell. When he surfaced, Lizzy was hanging over the edge, watching for him anxiously. He pushed wet hair from his face and forced himself not to eye her breasts.

"You scared me!" She stared at him in accusation, looking like a wild woman. Thanks to his hands, long strands of hair had escaped her thick braid in various places, giving her a woolly-headed look, like a damn red thistle. Her smooth cheeks were flushed, making the freckles more pronounced. Her lush mouth, which had felt so hot and hungry under his only moments before, was pressed into a severe line.

Gabe almost laughed. Hell, she wasn't even pretty, not really, and she sure as certain didn't have the right temperament to lure a man. So why had he reacted so strongly?

"Here." He handed her the shell, watched her sit back, bemused, to look it over. "It's just a mussel. The bottom of the lake is littered with them. I dated a girl for a while who used to find live ones and eat them raw."

Lizzy's head jerked up, and she dropped the shell. Her lip curled in a way that made her look ready to vomit. No, she looked far from pretty right now.

Gabe laughed out loud. "Gross, huh? I couldn't quite bring myself to kiss her again after that. I kept thinking of what had been in that mouth. Have you ever seen a live mussel? They're sort of slimy and gray."

She covered her mouth with a hand, swallowed hard, then sat back and glared at him some more. "Are you going to stay in there, or will you get out and answer my question?"

"Answer one for me first, okay?"

Her blue eyes widened, and he had to admit that they, at least, were beautiful. No matter her mood, her eyes were a focal point in her face, vivid and filled with curiosity and intelligence. He liked the color, dark and deep, unlike his faded, washed-out color. With the sun reflecting off the lake, he could see green and black and navy striations in her irises, lending richness to the unique color. As he studied her eyes, her pupils flared, reminding him how quickly she'd gotten aroused with him.

Arousing Little Red was fun, indeed. And from what he could tell, she could use a little fun in her life. Maybe it'd take some of the starch out of her spine and some of the vinegar out of her speech.

He propped his crossed arms over the edge of the dock, facing her and smiling into her stern face. "Where'd you get that suit?"

Bemused, she looked at herself, then at him. She plucked nervously at the material by her waist. "I...well, I hadn't owned a suit before this. You insisted we needed to swim, so I had to go get one last night. But I couldn't see spending a lot of money on one when this would likely be the only time I wore it. So I grabbed the cheapest one I could find."

"The cheapest one-piece?"

Her lips trembled, fascinating him. "I'm not exactly the type to wear a bikini."

"Why not?" His voice dropped despite his effort to sound dispassionate. "You have an incredible body, Lizzy." He was serious, but he could tell by the way her eyes darkened and she looked away that she didn't believe him.

"Lizzy?" She wouldn't look at him. His heart softened, felt too thick in his chest. Very gently he asked, "When was the last time you looked at yourself naked?"

Her head snapped up, her cheeks hectic with hot color. Her mouth opened twice, but nothing came out. Finally she glared and said with acerbity, "Why do you deliberately try to embarrass me? Is that your idea of fun, to make me feel...feel..."

"Feel what, sugar?" His hand was a scant inch from her small foot, and he caught her ankle, using his thumb to caress her arch. "Shy? You shouldn't. There's not a woman on this lake that looks better in her suit than you. Why don't you know that?"

Her auburn brows snapped down so fiercely, he expected her to get a headache. "I don't know what you're up to, Gabriel Kasper, but I'm not blind. I'm well aware of how I look, and if it wasn't for you and your ridiculous stipulations, I wouldn't be here now, sitting in this ridiculous suit!"

"You've enjoyed yourself," he felt compelled to remind her, then held on tight when she tried to draw her foot away.

"It was...unexpected." She looked prim and righteous, and he felt his blood heating in masculine reaction to her silent challenge. "As you've already surmised, I haven't done much kissing in my lifetime. I looked at this as sort of a...a learning experience."

Gabe grinned, his thumb still brushing sensually over her foot, making her stiffen. "So I'm sort of a class project, huh? Will you write another thesis? What I did over the summer vacation?"

Like a small volcano erupting, she jerked away and scrambled out of his reach. Her hands flattened on the dock to push herself upright, then she squealed and lifted a finger to her mouth.

Gabe watched her antics with curiosity. "What are you doing?"

"I'm leaving," she grumbled, still looking at her finger. "I realize now that you have no intention of answering my questions, and I can't afford to waste the time with you otherwise."

So he was a waste of time? Like hell! He'd make her eat those words. Gabe levered himself onto the dock, and his weight set it off kilter, causing Lizzy to tilt into him. Her attention was still on her finger.

"I'll answer your damn question, so quit frowning."

She gave him a skeptical, disbelieving look, then went back to frowning.

"What's wrong with you? Did you hurt yourself?" He leaned over her shoulder to see her hand, and as usual, she pulled it close to her chest as if protecting it from him.

"I have a splinter, thanks to you." As an afterthought, she added, "It hurts."

Gabe wrested her hand away from her body and looked at the injured finger. A jagged piece of wood was imbedded under the pad of her middle finger. "Damn. That sucker is huge."

She tried to pull her hand free. She did that constantly, he realized, always pulling away from him.

Well, not constantly. When he'd been kissing her, she'd strained against him.

"I can get it out."

"No!" She tugged again, finally gaining her release. "I can take care of it after I get home. If you're ready to leave?"

Gabe chewed the side of his mouth. "Actually, no, I'm not ready to leave. You have a question for me, and I'll answer it. But first let me take care of this."

"Gabe..."

"Stop being such a sissy. I won't hurt you."

Her chin firmed, her lips pursed, and then she thrust her hand toward him. "Fine. Do your worst."

Without hesitation, Gabe lifted her finger to his mouth. He heard Lizzy gasp, felt her tremble. Probing with his tongue, he located the end of the splinter, then carefully, gently closed his teeth around it. It pulled out easily.

He smiled at her, still with her hand close to his mouth. "There. That wasn't so bad, was it?"

She had that glazed look in her eyes again, like the one she'd had before the fishing boat had interrupted. Unable to help himself with her looking so flustered and shivering, he held her gaze and kissed her fingertip. Her pupils dilated, her lips parting. Damn, but she was quick to react—which made him react, too.

It was if they were connected by their gazes, an intimate hold that he'd never quite experienced before. Gabe touched the tip of his tongue to her finger and heard her inhalation of breath. Her eyes grew heavy, her lashes dipping down. He drew her finger into his mouth and sucked softly. With a moan, she closed her eyes.

Damn, it was erotic. *She* was erotic. Moving her finger along his bottom lip, he said, "Being in the water is second nature to me. It never scares me."

He was shocked by how husky his voice had become, but still, it jarred her enough that her eyes opened. Gabe dipped his tongue between her fingers, licked along the length of one. "I'm as at home in the water as I am on land. Especially this lake. I never once considered there was any danger to me, because there wasn't, so I wasn't afraid."

"Oh."

He moved to her thumb, drawing it into his mouth and tugging gently, just as he might with a breast. The thought inflamed him.

"After the kids and their mother were out of the way, I didn't have time to think or be afraid. I just reacted."

"I...I see."

Her voice was so low and rough he could barely understand her. She watched him through slitted eyes, her body swaying slightly. "I learned to drive boats when I was knee-high to a grasshopper. I started working on boat motors when I was ten, knew more about them than most grown men by the time I was fourteen."

He licked her palm, then the racing pulse in her wrist.

"Because I knew what I was doing, there was no danger, no reason to be afraid."

"I see."

Her eyes were closed, her free hand curled into a fist, her breasts heaving.

"Therefore," Gabe added, as he started to lower her once again, "I'm not what you'd call a hero at all."

Her back no sooner touched the dock than she bolted upright. Her head smacked his chin with the force of a prizefighter's blow. She blinked hard, rubbed her head and scowled at him.

After working his jaw to make certain she hadn't broken anything, Gabe asked, "Are you all right?"

"You've given me a concussion."

He smiled. "I have not." Then: "Why'd you get so jumpy?"

"I need to write everything down before I forget it."

Rolling his eyes, Gabe said, "So you're finally satisfied?" No sooner did the words leave his mouth than he looked at her spectacular breasts, saw her pointed nipples and knew true satisfaction was a long way off. Not that she'd ever admit it.

Her gaze downcast, she said simply, "I'm satisfied—for that question. But I have so many more." Looking at him, a soft plea in her gaze, she asked, "Will it really be so difficult to let me get some answers?"

Damn, he wanted her. He wanted to see that look on her face when she was naked beneath him. It defied reason and went against everything he knew about his preferences and inclinations. She was so far from the type of woman who usually caught his eye that it was almost laughable.

But it didn't change the facts.

Gabe chucked her chin. "I'm willing if you are."

"Meaning?"

There was a note of caution in her tone that made him smile with triumph. "Meaning as long as we stick to our original bargain, I'll answer your questions. One kiss per question."

Lizzy turned her head to stare at the lake. There was a stillness about her that he hadn't seen before, and it made him uneasy.

"Because this is important to me," she said without inflection, "I'll agree if you insist. But what we've just been doing...that was more than kissing." She turned her big blue eyes on him and added, "Wasn't it?"

Sure felt like more to him! But he'd never admit that to her. He had a feeling that if she knew how she'd turned him on, how close he'd gotten to losing all control, she'd never agree to see him again, much less let him kiss her. "It's not a big deal, Lizzy. You don't have to worry for your reputation or your chastity."

Her lips tightened, giving her a wounded look. Gabe cursed. He'd wanted to reassure her, not make light of their mutual attraction. "I didn't mean..."

"Why?" She turned to face him. "Why is it so important to you to toy with me?"

"I'm not toying with you, damn it."

She obviously didn't believe him. "Do you enjoy seeing me flustered, embarrassed? Do you enjoy knowing this is all very strange to me?"

A direct attack. He hadn't been expecting it, no more than he'd anticipated her vehemence. He watched her, but she once again avoided his gaze. After some thought, Gabe said honestly, "I like you. And it's for certain I like kissing you." She made an exasperated sound, but he continued. "You're different from the women I know around here."

"You mean I'm odd?"

He laughed at the suspicious accusation in her tone and look. "No, that's not what I mean. I've known most of the women in these parts for all of my life. They're entirely comfortable with me and with their own sexuality."

She slanted him a look. "I'm odd."

"No, you are not!" He tucked a long tendril of hair behind her ear, still smiling. "You're a...contradiction. Sweet and sassy—"

"What a sexist remark!"

"—and pushy but shy. You intrigue me. I guess it's tit for tat. Just as you seem to want to know what makes me tick, I want to know what makes you tick. It's as simple as that."

"It doesn't feel simple."

"That's because you're evidently not used to men paying you attention." She didn't answer his charge, and he frowned. Catching her chin and bringing her face around to his, he asked the question uppermost in his mind. "Why is that, Lizzy?"

She shook her head, her lips scrunched together.

"I figure you must be...what? Twenty-two?"

She looked at the sky. "Almost twenty-three."

"Yet you had no idea how to kiss. What girl gets through high school these days, much less college, without doing some necking?"

She glared at him and growled, "Redheaded, freckled, gangly girls who are shy and bookish, apparently."

Gabe took a telling perusal of her body. "Sweetheart, you're not gangly. Far from it."

She stared at him hard for at least three heartbeats, then asked with endearing caution, "Really?"

Tenderness swelled over him, taking him by surprise. "Didn't your mother ever tell you that you'd filled out real nice?"

She clasped her hands in her lap and shook her head. "My mother died when I was twelve."

Gabe scooted closer to her and put his arm around her sun warmed shoulders. He didn't question his need to hold her, to touch her. "Friends? Sisters?"

Shaking her head, she explained, "I'm an only child. And I didn't really have that many friends in school." As if admitting a grave sin, she added, "I was always very backward until recently."

Gabe squeezed her gently. "You're hardly a robust conqueror now."

"I know. It's not easy for me to do all these interviews, but they're important, so I do them." Her expression turned mocking. "Most of them have been fairly quick and simple."

"Then it's a good thing you ran into me, huh? Because lady, if anyone ever needed shaking up a little, it's you."

"I need to complete my thesis."

"You have the rest of summer break, right?"

She nodded warily, obviously uncertain of his intent.

"So why don't we indulge each other? I'll answer

any questions you have, and in return, you'll let me convince you how adorable you are in that bathing suit."

Her chin tucked in close to her chest. "Convince me...how?"

"By what we've already been doing. I won't ever push you further than you want to go, you have my word on that. But I can promise there'll be more kissing." His hand cradled her head. "You won't mind that so much, will you, Lizzy?"

She didn't reply to that, and she didn't look convinced. In a slightly choked voice that gave away her tension, she said, "I need you to be more specific than that."

Gabe chewed it over, trying to think of how to couch his terms so she would be reassured. "Okay, how's this. I'll answer a question and you'll cut loose a little, my choice of how. And before you start arguing, first I want you to go to a drive-in with me. You ever been to the drive-in?"

"With my father when I was young. I didn't even know they still had them."

"You're in for a treat!" *And I'm in for a little torture.* "We can go over to the next county, to the Dirty Dixie." He bobbed his eyebrows. "They play fairly raunchy movies—which will probably be another first for you, right?"

Looking dazed, she nodded.

"Perfect. How about this Friday? That's two days away, plenty of time for you to get used to the idea." *And plenty of time for him to get a better grip on himself.*

She hesitated once again and Gabe held his breath. Then she nodded. "All right. Where should I meet you?"

"Ah, no," he told her gently, knowing she wanted to keep him at a distance and knowing, too, that he wouldn't allow it. "You'll give me your address and phone number. I pick up the women I take on dates, Lizzy, I don't *meet* them."

She seemed to consider that, then shrugged in feigned indifference. Taking up her pencil, she jotted her address and phone number. Gabe accepted the scrap of paper, then slipped off the edge of the dock and waded to the boat to put it in his cooler for safe-keeping.

Lizzy, watching him in the water, said, "I'm renting the upstairs from this nice single mother. She has two young children and needed the extra money."

Gabe knew she was prattling out of nervousness. He hated to see an end to the day, but he checked his waterproof watch and saw it was time to go. "We'd better head back. I have some work to do."

"I thought you didn't have a job."

Looking at her from the other side of the boat, he gave her a wide grin. "Angling for another question? All right, I can be generous." He propped his fore-arms over the metal gunwale and explained, "I don't have a regular job, but I have more work than I can handle. I'm sort of a handyman and this time of year everyone needs something built, repaired or re-vamped. And that's all I'm telling you, so get that look out of your eyes."

"Spoilsport."

Gabe maneuvered the boat close to the dock. "Since I now know you're afraid of the water—something you should have told me right off—I'll be gallant and hold the boat steady for you to climb in."

"You won't expect me to get in the water again?"

He shook his head at her hopeful expression. "Oh, I imagine we'll get you used to it little by little. After all, what's the use of taking a vacation near a lake if you don't want to get wet? But for today you've had enough."

She couldn't quite hide her relief. "Thanks."

Using exaggerated caution, she scooted off the dock and into the boat. Gabe watched the way her long legs bent, how her breasts filled the snug suit, how her bottom settled neatly on the metal seat, heated by the sun.

Damn, he was in deep. And he couldn't even say why. In the normal course of things, a woman like Ms. Elizabeth Parks shouldn't have appealed to him at all. She was uptight, pushy, inexperienced...but she was also funny and curious and she had about the sweetest body he'd ever seen.

With a muttered curse against his fickle libido, Gabe hauled himself over the side of the boat, which made her squeal and grab the seat with a death grip. "You can thank me Friday night," he told her, and wondered if he'd be able to keep his hands off her even then. Two days didn't seem like near enough time to get himself together.

But it did seem like an eternity when already he wanted her so bad his hands were shaking.

GABE FELT THE SUN on his shoulders, smelled the
newly mown grass and breathed a deep sigh of contentment. Or at least, he'd be content if he could get a
redheaded wonder out of his head. He steered the
tractor mower toward the last strip of high grass by
rote. He and his brothers had so much property, they
only kept up the acres surrounding the house. Beyond that, the land was filled with wild shrubs and
colorful flowers and mature trees of every variety. It
was gorgeous in the fall, when the leaves changed
color, but Gabe liked summer best.

His mother used to accuse him of being part lizard,
because the heat seldom bothered him, and he was always drawn to the sunshine.

Life had been different since his two oldest brothers had married. Different in a very nice way. He enjoyed having Honey around. She made the house feel
homier in some small indefinable ways, like the smell
of her scented candles in the bathroom after she'd
been indulging in a long soak, or the way she always
hugged him when he left the house, cautioning him
to be careful—as if he ran around risking his neck
whenever he went out the door.

Gabe grinned. He could still recall how Honey had
cried when Morgan had moved to his own house.
Never mind that it was just up the hill; she liked having all the brothers as near as possible. It was a huge
bonus that Morgan had married her sister, Misty. The
two women were very close and managed to get together every day, especially since Misty had given
birth to an adorable little girl seven months ago. Amber Marie Hudson was about the most precious thing

he'd ever seen. And watching his brother fuss over the baby was an endless source of entertainment.

Females flat-out fascinated Gabe, whether they were seven months, twenty-seven or seventy. He didn't think he'd ever tire of learning more about them.

He was pondering what he might learn from a certain redhead when he saw a car pull into their long drive. Gabe stopped the tractor and watched, a feeling of foreboding creeping up his sweaty back. The car, a small purple Escort, looked suspiciously like the one he'd seen Lizzy park at the docks. He'd noticed because the purple clashed so loudly with her hair.

And sure enough, even from this distance, when she stepped out of the car, there was no mistaking the fiery glint of the sun off her bright head.

Scowling, he put the tractor in gear and headed toward the house. He was aware of a strange pounding in his chest, hoping to intercept her before any of his brothers saw her. Or worse, before Honey or Misty saw her.

But his hopes were vain. Just as he neared the drive the front door opened and there stood Honey, her long blond hair moving gently in the breeze, her killer smile in place.

Oh, hell.

He watched in horror as Lizzy was evidently invited in, as she accepted and as the door closed behind her. The tractor was too damn slow so he stopped it, turned it off and ran the rest of the way.

His chest was heaving and he was dripping sweat

by the time he bolted through the front door. No one was in sight. He hurried down the hallway to the family room, finding it empty. He stopped, trying to listen. A feminine laugh caught his attention, and he raced for the kitchen. He had to stop her before she said too much, before she started in with her questions—before anyone found out he'd been kissing her....

He skidded to a halt on the tile floor. The kitchen was crowded, what with Honey and her sister and Amber and Sawyer... Gabe stared at Lizzy, seated at the table with her back to him.

Sawyer was looking her over—not politely, but in minute detail. He leaned over Lizzy with his fingers grazing her cheek, so close to her she could probably feel his breath, for God's sake.

Gabe's brows snapped down to match Sawyer's frown, and he demanded, "What the hell is going on?"

Everyone looked up. Honey was the first to speak, saying, "Gabe. I was just about to come get you."

Misty shook her head at him in a pitying way, as if he'd gotten himself into trouble somehow, and Amber cooed at the sound of his voice. Gabe ignored them all to stare at his oldest brother.

Of course Lizzy would have to call at lunchtime, he thought darkly, when everyone was bound to be around. Normally Sawyer would have been in his office at the back of the house, treating patients. Luckily, to his mind, Jordan always ate lunch in town. Morgan used to, too, until he married Misty. Now he was likely to show up any minute. Gabe needed to get Lizzy out of the house before she said too much about their association. He could imagine the ribbing he'd take if his brothers knew he was interested in— as in majorly turned on by—a prickly little redheaded witch with freckles!

His face heated at the mere thought.

Then Lizzy turned to look at him, and he knew the heat in his face was nothing compared to hers.

His frown intensified, but for different reasons, as he drifted closer, studying her every feature. "Damn, Lizzy, what happened?"

She was bright pink with sunburn, her nose red, her soft mouth slightly puffy. Without thinking about his rapt audience, he knelt in front of her chair and smoothed a wayward tendril of hair gently behind her ear. God, even the tops of her ears were red!

She licked her lips, looking horribly embarrassed and glancing around at the others. "I'm fine, Gabe," she murmured, trying to get him to stand up while sneaking glances at his family. "There's no reason for this fuss."

He paid no attention at all to her words, too intent on discovering every speck of skin that had been reddened. "I thought you had sunscreen on yesterday."

"I did," she assured him, looking more wretchedly miserable by the minute. "I guess it wasn't strong enough, or maybe it washed off in the water."

Sawyer made an impatient sound, recalling Gabe to the fact that he was on his knees in front of Lizzy, treating her like the most precious woman in the world. He jerked to his feet, but he still couldn't take his concerned gaze off her. "Does it hurt?"

"No." She tried a weak smile, then flinched. "Truly. I'm fine."

Sawyer rudely pushed Gabe aside. "I'm going to give you some topical ointment for the sting. In the meantime, stay out of the sun—" and here he glared at Gabe "—and wear very loose clothes. It doesn't look like you'll blister, but I'd say you're going to be plenty uncomfortable for the next few days."

Honey stepped up with some folded paper towels soaked in cool tea. "This'll help. I'm fair-skinned, too, and it's always worked for me."

Misty leaned close to watch as Honey patted the towels gently in place on Elizabeth's bare shoulders. Gabe realized that Lizzy wore a shapeless white cotton dress, so long it hung to her ankles. He looked closely and could see by the soft fullness beneath the bodice that she wasn't wearing a bra. His heart skipped a beat.

She'd said she never went braless, and her breasts were so firm and round, he believed her. The sunburn must indeed be painful for her to go without one.

To distract himself, he looked around the room and settled on smiling at the baby. At his attention, Amber flailed her pudgy arms from her pumpkin seat on the table, gurgling and blowing spit bubbles. Gabe laughed. "Sorry, kiddo. I'm too sweaty to hold you right now."

Elizabeth watched as he reached out and tweaked the baby's toe, and he knew she was planning on putting that into her little notebook, too. He scowled.

Morgan stepped in through the kitchen door and

went immediately to Misty, lifting her into a bear hug that led to a lingering, intimate kiss. The way Misty continued to flush at her husband's touch always tickled Gabe. Morgan had been well and fully tamed.

He turned and hauled Amber out of her chair and against his chest, then nuzzled the baby's downy black hair. Amber squealed as he settled her in the crook of his arm.

Only then did Morgan notice Elizabeth. One dark brow shot up. "Hello."

Misty shook the dreamy look off her face and smiled. "Morgan, this is Elizabeth Parks, a friend of Gabe's."

Morgan's enigmatic gaze transferred to Gabe, and Gabe felt his face heat again. "She looks done to a crisp, Gabe. I suppose you weren't...ah, paying attention to the sun? Had your mind on...other things?"

Gabe stiffened and said, "You know I can't hit you while you're holding the baby. Care to give her to her mother?"

"Nope." He kissed the baby's tiny ear and with a grin turned to Elizabeth. "Nice to meet you, Elizabeth."

She nodded. "And you, Sheriff."

"You're joining us for lunch?"

"Oh. No, please. I just... I'm sorry to impose. Really." Her attention flicked nervously to Gabe as all his interfering relatives assured her she was no imposition at all. "I just had a few questions, if you have the time."

Morgan pulled out a chair. "Questions about what?"

Gabe stepped forward before she could answer. "Lizzy, I'd like to talk to you. In private."

She stalled, staring at him with a guilty expression.

Sawyer nudged him aside. "I've only got fifteen minutes left before I have to see a patient. You can wait that long, can't you, Gabe?"

He wanted to say no, he damn well couldn't wait, but he knew that would only stir up more speculation. So instead he took the cool towels from Honey and began placing them on Lizzy's shoulders. A thought struck him, and he looked at her feet, set together primly beneath the long skirt. She wore thick white socks and slip-on shoes.

He gave her an exasperated look. "Your feet are burned, too, I suppose?"

Not since he'd met her had Lizzy been so withdrawn. She kept her wide eyes trained on him and nodded. In a tiny voice, she admitted, "A little."

Gabe knelt and very carefully pried off her loose loafers, then peeled the socks off her feet. Like a wet hen, Lizzy fussed and complained and tried to shoo him away. He persisted, despite Morgan's choked laugh and Sawyer's hovering attention.

Her feet were small and slender. Looking at how red they were, Gabe had the awful urge to kiss them better, and instead looked at her with a warning in his gaze. "You should be at home, naked, instead of running around all over the place, asking your crazy questions."

Honey gasped. Morgan guffawed, making Amber bounce in delight. Misty smacked Gabe's shoulder.

But Sawyer agreed. "He's right. Wearing clothes

right now is just going to aggravate the sunburn. Taking cool baths and using plenty of aloe, and some ibuprofen for the pain, is the best thing you could do for yourself right now." He glared at Gabe. "Of course if baby brother here had remembered that not everyone is a sun worshiper with skin like leather, there wouldn't be a problem."

Gabe gritted his teeth. "I'm well aware of how delicate a woman's skin is. I thought she had sunscreen on. Besides, we weren't really out in the sun that long."

Lizzy stirred uncomfortably. "Gabe's right. This is my fault, not his. I guess I hadn't counted on the sun's reflection off the lake being so strong."

"Water does magnify the sun," Sawyer agreed, then propped his hands on his hips and asked in his best physician's voice, "Are you burned anywhere else?"

Lizzy shook her head and at the same time said, "Just my legs." But as Gabe started to lift her skirt she slapped his hands away. Her tone was both horrified and embarrassed. "Don't even think it!"

He grinned. She was behaving more like herself, and he was vastly relieved. He didn't like seeing her so quiet and apprehensive. "Sorry. Just trying to see how bad it is."

She scowled. "Mostly on my knees, and you can just take my word on that, Gabriel Kasper."

Morgan leaned back in his seat, both brows lifted. Everyone stared at them, transfixed. Gabe remembered what he was doing and came to his feet again.

How the hell did he keep ending up on his knees in front of her?

After setting a platter of sandwiches on the table, Honey said, "Join us for lunch, okay? What would you like to drink? I have tea and lemonade and—"

"Oh, no. Really, I didn't mean to catch you at a bad time." Lizzy reached for the towels on her shoulders, meaning to remove them. "I can just come back another time if you agree to a short interview."

Gabe let out a gust of relief. "That's a good idea. Come on, I'll walk you to your car."

But Lizzy hadn't even gotten the first towel removed before everyone rejected her intentions and insisted she stay. Hell, they *begged* her to stay, the nosy pests.

Well, they could do as they pleased, Gabe decided, but that didn't mean he had to stick around and take part in it. "I'm going to go shower," he announced, and of course, that was just fine and dandy. No one begged *him* to stick around! Irritated, he stomped out of the room, but before he'd even rounded the corner, he heard Morgan start chuckling, and before long, they were all laughing hysterically.

Everyone but Lizzy.

5

ELIZABETH BIT her lip, not sure what was so funny. She hoped they weren't laughing at her, but then Honey gave her a big smile and said, "Gabe is so amusing sometimes."

Elizabeth had no idea how she meant that, and she didn't ask. She cleared her throat and said, "I'm doing a thesis on heroes for my college major. I've been working on it for some time, and I'd just about finished, then I heard about the boating incident here last summer and decided to add Gabriel to my notes."

Morgan tilted his head. "What boating incident?"

That set her back. His own brother wasn't aware of what had happened? But Misty waved a hand and explained to her husband, "I'm sure she's talking about Gabe saving that woman and her children, right?"

Elizabeth nodded.

"That was right after our wedding. Morgan wasn't paying much attention to what happened around him back then."

Morgan gave his wife a smoldering look. "You're to blame for that, Malone, not me. Can I help it if you're distracting?"

Honey laughed. "Stop it, you two, or you'll embarrass our guest." She sat herself on her husband's lap, and Sawyer wrapped his arms around her. "Gabe is a real sweetheart, Elizabeth. We just enjoy teasing him a little."

Elizabeth could attest to the sweetheart bit. From what she'd found out so far, there didn't live a finer example of the term *lady's man*. She cleared her throat. "So you *do* remember the event?"

"Sure." Honey settled comfortably against her husband's wide chest. To Elizabeth's amazement, Sawyer Hudson managed to eat that way, as if having his wife on his lap was a common occurrence. He quickly devoured three sandwiches, which was one less than Morgan ate. Misty and Honey each nibbled on a half. Since they were insistent, Elizabeth took a bite of one herself. She hadn't realized she was hungry until then.

The sunburn had made her so miserable she'd only wanted to find something to do, to keep her mind off it. Her skin felt too tight, itchy and burning. Clothes were a misery—Sawyer Hudson was right about that. But she simply wasn't used to parading around naked and had decided to take her mind off it by finding out more about Gabe before their trip to the movies.

"Can you tell me about it?" Elizabeth asked after a large drink of icy lemonade. With the cool towels on her shoulders and the uncomfortable shoes off her feet, she felt much better.

"Sure." Honey looked thoughtful for a moment, then turned to Morgan. "You ended up arresting the driver of that boat, right?"

Morgan growled, his tone so threatening that Elizabeth jumped. "The fool was drunk and could have damn well killed somebody. If it had been up to me, he'd have lost not only his boating license, but his driver's license, as well. As it turned out, though, he was banned from the lake, got a large fine and spent a week in jail. Hell, that poor woman was so shook up, Sawyer had to give her a sedative."

Sawyer nodded and his tone, in comparison to Morgan's was solemn. "She thought one or both of her kids would be hurt. She was almost in shock." Then he smiled. "When I got there, I found Gabe with a kid in his arms, one wrapped around his leg, and the woman gushing all over him. The look of relief on Gabe's face when he spotted me was priceless."

Elizabeth reached for her bag on the floor by her chair and extracted her notebook and pencil. "Can you describe it for me?"

"What?"

"The look on his face."

Sawyer appeared startled by her request, then shrugged. "Sure."

IT WAS ONLY fifteen minutes before Gabe rejoined them, his shaggy blond hair still wet and hanging in small ringlets on the back of his neck, his requisite cutoffs clean and dry. Elizabeth had already taken page after page of notes, supplied by all the family members, and she was ecstatic to finally have someone agree with her that Gabriel Kasper's actions had, in fact, been heroic.

When Gabe saw her notebook out, he glared and stomped over to snag the last sandwich on the platter.

Elizabeth drew in a deep breath as he leaned past her, but all she could smell was soap. When Gabe had entered earlier, the earthy scent of damp male flesh warm from the sunshine had clung to him—an enticing aphrodisiac. That wonderfully potent scent, combined with the sight of him, had made her nearly too breathless to talk. She hadn't thought she'd see him today. When she'd called the number Bear gave her, Honey had told her Gabe would be working all day. Elizabeth hadn't realized she meant working around his own home.

She also hadn't realized they'd all make such a fuss about her sunburn. She felt like an idiot for getting burned in the first place. She, better than anyone, knew how easily the sun affected her. She'd even brought along the sunscreen to apply often, keeping it in her bag. But she'd been sidetracked by Gabe and kissing and the erotic feelings he'd engendered. She hadn't thought once about overexposure.

Honey stood to make more sandwiches since Morgan had started prowling around for a cookie and Gabe had only gotten one sandwich. Once his lap was vacated, Sawyer excused himself, saying he'd go fetch the aloe cream he wanted Lizzy to use.

Gabe downed a tall glass of iced tea, and Elizabeth watched his throat work, saw the play of muscles in his arms and shoulders as he tipped his head back. He lowered the glass, caught her scrutiny and frowned at her. He opened his mouth to say something, but at that moment, Morgan thrust the baby into Gabe's arms and he got distracted by a tiny fist grabbing his chest hair.

The contrast between Gabe, so big, so strong, golden blond and tanned, and the tiny dark-haired baby held securely in his arms made Elizabeth's chest feel too tight. She'd have thought a man like him, a Lothario with only hedonistic pleasures on his mind, wouldn't have been so confident while holding an infant. But Gabe not only held the baby without hesitation, he blew raspberries on her soft belly and nibbled on her tiny toes.

Elizabeth decided it was time to make a strategic retreat. She knew, despite his gentle touch with the baby, that he was angry with her. She supposed that negated her deal with him; there'd be no movies at the drive-in. But at least, she told herself, trying to be upbeat instead of despondent, she'd gotten what she wanted. She had an entire notebook full of details, and hadn't that been her single goal all along?

Sawyer reappeared with a large tube of ointment and handed it to Elizabeth. "Put that on every hour or so, or whenever your skin feels uncomfortable. It's mostly aloe. You can keep it in the refrigerator if you like. Drink as much water as you can—rehydrating your skin will help it feel more comfortable. Oh, and take cool baths, not showers. Showers are too stressful to the damaged skin. If it doesn't feel better by tomorrow evening, give me a call, okay?"

Feeling horribly conspicuous, Elizabeth nodded. "How much do I owe you for the cream?"

"Not a thing. I'll take it out of Gabe's hide later."

Since Gabe smirked at that, Elizabeth assumed it

was a joke. "Thank you." She glanced at Gabe, then away. "For everything."

Sawyer kissed his wife, his niece and his sister-in-law, then went off to work again. They were a demonstrative lot, always hugging and patting and kissing. It disconcerted her.

Misty and Honey and Gabe all walked her to the door. Gabe was deathly quiet, which she felt didn't bode well since he was usually joking and teasing. As she stepped onto the porch, Honey said, "Misty and I are having lunch in town tomorrow. Would you like to join us? The restaurant where Misty works part-time has fabulous beef stew on Friday afternoons. And afterward, we can all go to the library. I know they must have kept records of the local paper there on file. You could see the firsthand reports of Gabe's—" she glanced at her brother-in-law with a wicked smile "—daring feat."

Gabe gave Honey a look that promised retribution, but she just laughed and hugged him.

Misty added, "It'll be fun."

Aware of Gabe spearing her with his hot gaze, knowing he expected her to turn the women down, Elizabeth nonetheless nodded. "All right. Thank you."

She could have sworn she heard Gabe snarling.

Misty took the baby from Gabe's arms. "Great. If you know where the diner is, we could meet you there at eleven."

"That'll be fine."

"Perfect. We'll see you then!"

Misty and Honey retreated together, and suddenly

Elizabeth wished they were still there. Gabe looked ready for murder.

It was his own fault, she decided, refusing to cower. She raised her chin, gave him a haughty look and turned toward her car. Gabe stalked along beside her.

"What are you doing here, Red?"

Uh-oh. He really was angry. "In each of my studies, I've included the accountings of family members whenever possible."

"But you and I had a deal."

Had. She was right, the deal was no longer valid. Disappointment swamped her, but she fought it off. It had been foolish to look forward to her time with Gabe. He was the epitome of a town playboy. He'd amuse himself with her while she was in town, and when she left he'd never think of her.

But she knew already she'd never be able to forget him. Pathetic, she decided, and deliberately tamped down her regret. She opened the car door and tossed in her bag. She hadn't been able to carry it with the strap over her shoulder because of the burn. She was anxious to follow Sawyer's advice and get naked. Her clothes felt like sandpaper against her sensitive skin.

Gabe watched her closely and she managed a shrug. "You never told me I couldn't talk with your family."

"Bull." He leaned closer, crowding her by putting one hand on the roof of her car, the other at the top of the door frame. "You knew damn good and well I didn't want you snooping around. That's why I agreed to answer your questions myself."

With him so close, her heart thundered. Memories washed over her and her belly tingled in response. She couldn't seem to stop staring at his mouth and swallowed hard. "I understand. If...if you want to cancel the rest of it, I won't argue with you."

Gabe stiffened. "Cancel the rest of what?"

The hair on his chest was still slightly damp, as if he'd dried in a hurry. She'd never in her life known a man who paraded around in such a state of undress almost continually. She didn't think he was deliberately flaunting himself for her benefit so much as he was totally at ease with his own body, aware he had no reason for shame or reserve. She curled her hands into fists to keep from touching him.

"The...the drive-in, the...having fun and loosening up." Pride made her add, "I thought it was a dumb plan all along."

He tipped up her chin with an extremely gentle touch. "Oh, no, you don't," he growled. "You're not backing out on me, Lizzy."

"But..." She faltered, caught by the intensity in his gaze. "You're angry."

"Damn right. And we'll discuss my anger tomorrow. At the movies. If you think I'm going to let you breach our deal now, especially after all your damn snooping, you've got another thing coming."

"Oh." Elizabeth couldn't think of anything else to say. Relief was a heavy throbbing in her breasts. "Okay."

Once again she stared at his mouth and felt her lips trembling in remembrance of how he'd kissed her, how he'd tasted, how hot his mouth had been.

Breathless again, she whispered, "Gabe?" and even she could hear the longing in the single word.

Gabe's nostrils flared and suddenly he cursed. He leaned forward and took her mouth with careful hunger, that single rough finger beneath her chin holding her captive. The kiss was long and deep and Elizabeth grabbed his shoulders, though he didn't return the embrace. His tongue thrust in, hot and wet, and she accepted it, stroking it with her own, moaning softly.

When Gabe lifted his head a scant inch, she said, "Oh, my."

He smiled. "Yeah." There was a husky catch in his voice.

She realized she was practically hanging on him and jerked back. "I didn't mean—"

Again Gabe touched her chin, making her meet his eyes. "You can believe I'd have had you close, Lizzy, if I wasn't afraid of hurting you." His voice dropped and he asked, "Are your thighs burned?"

She couldn't seem to get enough oxygen into her lungs. "A little."

"Your arms?"

"Some."

His mouth barely touched hers. "Your breasts?"

She drew a shuddering breath. "Just..." She sounded like a bullfrog and cleared her throat. "Just the very tops, where the suit didn't cover."

"Want some help with that cream?"

New heat washed over her, making her light-headed. "No! I can manage just fine on my own."

His mouth twitched with a grin. "Spoilsport."

"I should go." She should go before she begged him to help her with the cream, before she attacked his mostly naked body. Before she made a total fool of herself. She had to remember that to Gabe, this was just a game, a way to pass the time while indulging her curiosity. He wasn't serious about any of it. As far as she could tell, he wasn't overly serious about anything.

"All right." Gabe straightened, then gave her another frown. "Don't think I'm not mad over you showing up here. But we'll talk about it when I pick you up for the drive-in, when I'll be assured of a little privacy."

No sooner did he say it than he looked struck by that thought and twisted to look behind him. Elizabeth peered over his shoulder just in time to see a curtain drop and several heads duck out of sight. Gabe cursed.

Unable to believe what she'd seen, Elizabeth asked, "They were spying on you?"

Gabe looked livid but accepting. "Don't sound so incredulous. I'd have done the same."

"You would have?"

"Sure." Then he laughed and scrubbed both hands over his face. "Oh, hell, the cat's out of the bag now. I'm never going to hear the end of it."

"The end of what?" Surely he wasn't embarrassed because he'd been a hero. That didn't make any sense at all.

"Never mind." He turned to her, shaking his head. "Maybe I should just do like Morgan and build my own place. 'Course, Honey'd probably have a fit."

Elizabeth had a hard time keeping up with his switches in topic.

Gabe pointed toward a spot on a hill overlooking the main house. "See that house up there? That's Morgan's. He and Misty moved in there last year. Until then, we all lived in the house together. Morgan lived in the main part of the house with Sawyer and his son, Casey. Have you met Case yet? No? Well, you're in for a treat. Hell of a kid."

She reached for her notebook to jot down the name, but Gabe caught her wrist with a sigh. "Forget I said that. Leave Casey alone."

"But you said..."

"You've done enough meddling, Red."

There was definite menace in his tone. Elizabeth committed the name to memory, determined to write it down as soon as she was away from Gabe. To distract him, she said, "Tell me about these living arrangements."

He gave her a narrow look, then shook his head. "Why not? There's no secret there. I live in the basement. I have my own entrance and it's nicer than most apartments. Jordan lives in the rooms over the garage."

Elizabeth frowned. "Four grown men all live together?"

"Yeah." Gabe squinted against the sun, then his eyes widened and he cursed. "Damn it, here I am, keeping you out in the sun again! Woman, don't you have any sense at all? Get on home."

"But—"

"No buts. I'll give you a family history on Friday.

After I explain how disgruntled I am with you for trespassing with my family."

Elizabeth huffed. "I didn't trespass. Honey invited me over."

"Yeah, I just bet she did."

Elizabeth sat carefully in the car, trying not to scrape her tender flesh on the seats. Gabe closed her door for her, then leaned in to give her another quick kiss. "Drive careful. And when you get home, get naked."

"Gabe," she admonished, embarrassed by his frank suggestion. She wondered if she'd ever get used to him.

She started the engine and put the car in reverse. Gabe leaned in the window once more. "And Elizabeth?"

She paused. Gabe stared at her unconfined breasts in the loose dress, then whispered, "When you're naked, think of me, okay?" He touched the end of her nose and sauntered away.

Elizabeth stared after him, goggle-eyed and flushed, her heart pounding so hard she could hear it—and dead certain that she'd do exactly as he had asked her to.

GABE CURSED HIMSELF the entire way there, but he couldn't make himself not go. He tried to talk himself out of it. He'd even made other plans—then had to cancel them.

He was worried about her, and damned if that wasn't a first. He'd never had a woman consume his thoughts so completely.

But the sunburn was his fault and he felt responsible. Plus he'd yelled at her and she was so sensitive, so inexperienced, she probably felt bad because of it. Besides, he wanted to know what his damn meddling brothers had told her, because they hadn't given him so much as a clue. Even Misty and Honey were staying mum, refusing to reveal a single word.

Gabe squeezed the steering wheel tight and called himself three kinds of a fool, because the bare-bones truth of it was that he wanted to see her. There. He'd admitted it. He liked her and he wanted her.

He pulled into the driveway on the quiet suburban street just outside of Buckhorn County and turned off the ignition. The house was an older redbrick two-story with mature trees and a meticulously trimmed lawn. As he got out of the car, Gabe wondered if Elizabeth had done as ordered and stripped down. Was she naked right now? Maybe lounging in a soothing tub of cool water?

He shoved his hands into his pockets and climbed the outside stairwell to the upper floor at the side of the building. Miniblinds were pulled shut over the only full-size window. That was good, he thought, just in case she was naked.

Gabe rocked on his heels, took a deep breath and knocked. There was no answer. Briefly he considered turning away in case she was asleep. But it was still early, not quite nine o'clock, so he knocked again, harder.

A muffled sound reached him from the other side of the door, and then he heard Lizzy call, "Who is it?"

She didn't sound as if she'd just awakened, but she

did sound wary. Probably she didn't get that many callers, especially not at night.

He felt a curious satisfaction at that deduction. "It's me, Red. Open up."

There were more muffled sounds, and finally the door opened the tiniest bit. One big blue eye peeked at him through the crack in the door. "Gabe. What in the world are you doing here?"

Rather than answer that, because he had no answer, he said, "Did I wake you?"

"Oh. No, I was just... Is anything wrong?"

"Yeah." He pushed against the door, and she hastily stepped out of the way. "I wanted to check... on...you." Gabe stared. His gut clenched and his toes curled. Lizzy had her hair all piled up on top of her head, and she wore only a sheet wrapped around her breasts. Loosely. Very loosely. In fact, if it wasn't for one small, tightly clenched fist, the sheet would have fallen. And good riddance, Gabe thought.

He shoved her front door shut with his heel. He knew he should say something, but he just kept staring.

Lizzy cleared her throat. "I was getting ready to put on some more of that ointment your brother gave me. It helps a lot, but it doesn't last all that long."

Gabe looked past her to the open kitchen nook. On the table sat a bowl of water and the tube of ointment Sawyer had given her. "I'll help you."

Her eyes flared wide. She shook her head, making that huge pile of hair threaten to topple. Her shoulders were bright pink, but just on the top, thank goodness. Most of her back, from what he could tell, was fine. But her breasts... Gabe swallowed. The sheet was white and damp in places around her chest; she must have been putting on cool compresses, he decided.

He was a man. He'd act like a man. Gabe put his arm around her sheet-covered waist and steered her toward the tiny kitchen. Her living room was minuscule, holding only a sofa, a single chair and some shelves. A thirteen-inch television was centered on the shelves and around that were some plants. The only other things in the spartan rented room were a few books and two photos. He'd check out the photos later, but for now he wanted to help ease her discomfort.

Her feet were bare and looked adorable peeking out from beneath the sheet. Pink, but adorable. Gabe looked at her breasts again, surreptitiously, so she wouldn't notice. The tops of her breasts, from just beneath her collarbone to somewhere beneath that white sheet, were sunburned.

"Here, sit down."

She remained standing. "Gabe, I'm perfectly capable of taking care of this myself."

"But why should you when I can help? I know it can't be easy to reach your shoulders."

Her mouth twisted, her eyes downcast. Her long auburn lashes left shadows on her cheeks from the fluorescent light overhead. He wanted to kiss her.

"I'll get dressed."

"Don't."

She stared at him, unblinking.

"Please, Lizzy?" He kept his tone cajoling, soothing. "Sit down and let me help, okay? It'll make *me* feel better, I promise."

Still she hesitated, and finally she heaved a sigh. "Oh, all right." She lowered herself carefully into the straight-back chair. "But if you hurt me," she warned, "I'm going to be really angry."

His hands shook as he stared at her shoulders. "I'll be as gentle as I can."

He lifted the tube of cream and realized it was cool. Lizzy must have been keeping it in the refrigerator, just as Sawyer had suggested. He squeezed a large dollop onto his fingertips, then very carefully began smoothing it over her skin. Her head dropped forward and she shivered.

"Cold?"

"It's supposed to be."

"I'm not hurting you?" Her skin was so delicate, even without the sunburn.

"No."

There was a tiny quaking to her voice that made everything masculine in him sit up and take notice. Velvety soft curls on the back of her neck got in his way, and he used one hand to lift them while spreading the cream with the other. Her neck was long and graceful, her hair somewhat lighter here, more like a golden strawberry blond. "Feel better?"

"Mm. Yes."

Gabe looked at her arms, saw they were pink and stepped to her side. He lifted her arm and said, "Brace your hand on my abdomen."

She jerked her hand as if he'd suggested she cut it

off. She held it protectively to her chest so he couldn't take it again.

Gabe smiled. "C'mon, Lizzy. Don't be shy. I just want to put the cream on you, and I'm even wearing a shirt. There's no reason to act so timid."

Her spine stiffened. "I am not acting timid! I'm just not used to how you...how you constantly..."

He could imagine what she'd eventually come up with, so he decided to help her. "How informal and comfortable and at ease I am? Yeah, that's true. Touching someone isn't a sin, sweetheart." He pried her arm loose, being careful not to hurt her, then pressed her hand to his abdomen. His muscles were clenched rock hard, not on purpose, but in startling reaction to the feel of her small hand there. "See. That's not so bad, is it?"

A tiny squeak.

Gabe lifted a brow, still covering her hand with his so she couldn't retreat. "What was that?"

Lizzy glared at him and said, "No. It's not...awful."

Laughing, Gabe released her and reached for the cream. "Now just hold still."

He could feel her trembling as he spread the sticky aloe cream up and down her slender arm. She felt so soft, so female, which he supposed made sense. It even made sense that his overcharged male brain immediately began to imagine how soft she was in other, more feminine places, like her inner thighs, her belly and lower.

He felt himself hardening and wanted to curse.

Like a doomed man, he continued with his ministrations, torturing himself, but enjoying it all the same.

With only one hand to hold it, her sheet started to slip. Gabe froze as she made a frantic grab for it, his breath held, but she managed to maintain her modesty.

Sighing, he went to her other side, determined to behave himself. He was not a boy ready to take his first woman. He was experienced, mature... There was absolutely no reason for all the anticipation, all the keen tension.

His voice gruff, he said, "You know the drill."

She looked away from him even as she thrust out her arm. Nervously, she said, "I have to admit I'm a little surprised to see you so fully dressed. I was beginning to think you didn't own any shirts or slacks."

He looked at his white T-shirt and faded jeans. The jeans were so old, so worn, they fit like a second skin—which meant that if she bothered to look at all, she'd see he had an erection. Again.

But of course she didn't look. Gabe studied her averted face and smiled. "Are you disappointed that I came fully clothed, Lizzy?"

In prim tones, she replied, "Not at all."

He didn't quite believe her. Sure, he felt the tension, but then, so did she. She was practically vibrating with it. Yet she'd deny any attraction. Most women came on to him with force; this tactic was totally unusual...and intriguing.

She turned her face even more, until her chin almost hit the chair back. Gabe bit his lip to keep from laughing. Elizabeth Parks was about the most entertaining woman he'd ever met. It was probably a good thing she wouldn't be here long or he'd get addicted to her prickly ways.

But until she left, he told himself, he might as well put them both out of their misery.

6

ELIZABETH DIDN'T quite know what to think when Gabe moved in front of her, insinuating his body into the small space between the Formica table and the chair where she sat. Every one of her nerve endings felt sensitized from the way he'd so gently stroked her. And now his lap was on a level with her gaze.

Her eyes widened. *He was turned on!* It wasn't just *her* feeling so sexually charged. But unlike Gabe, she was the only one uncertain how to continue, or if she even should.

Gabe leaned very close and gripped the seat of the chair in his large hands. Elizabeth yelped when he lifted it and moved it far enough for him to kneel in front of her. Her heart beat so hard she felt slightly sick, her vision almost blurring.

He smelled of aftershave mingled with his own unique scent. Never in her life had she noticed a man's smell before. She wished she could bottle Gabe's particular aroma—she'd make a fortune. There couldn't be a woman alive who wouldn't love his enticing scent.

His lips grazed her ears and he said softly, "I'm going to finish putting the cream on you, then we're going to do a little experimenting, all right?"

The soft, damp press of his mouth on her temple

served as a period to his statement. He phrased his comment as a question, but given the heat suffusing her, it had to be rhetorical.

Her hands opened and closed fitfully on the sheet. "What exactly do you mean?"

Leaning back on his haunches, Gabe stared at her and caught the hem of the sheet. "Your legs are burned, too." His rough palms slid up the back of her calves all the way to her knees, baring them as the sheet parted.

Elizabeth pressed herself back in the chair, her legs tightly clenched together, her toes curled. Good Lord, surely he didn't mean...

The sheet fell open over her thighs, barely leaving her modesty intact. She tried to hold it closed at her breasts and still push his hands away, but Gabe wasn't having it.

"Shhh. Shh, Lizzy, it's all right." He held perfectly still, not moving, not rushing her, waiting for her to calm down and either acquiesce or reject him.

"You're looking at me!" she said, not really wanting him to stop but unable to contain her embarrassment.

"Just your legs, sweetheart. And I've already seen them, right?"

She sucked in a quick, semicalming breath. He was right, in a way. "It just...it feels different."

"Because you're naked beneath the sheet?" His fingers continued to stroke up and down her calves, pausing occasionally to gently explore the back of her knees with a touch so gentle, so hot.

She'd had no idea the back of a knee could be an erogenous zone!

Gabe watched her, waiting for an answer. She forced the words past the constriction in her throat. "Yes, because I'm naked beneath the sheet."

"Am I hurting you, Lizzy?"

She shook her head, heated by the tone of his voice, the careful way he was treating her.

"Do you like this?" He began stroking her again, avoiding her sunburned areas while finding places that were ultrasensitive but nonthreatening.

His hands were so large, so dark against her paler complexion. Working hands, she thought stupidly, rough and callused. She gulped. Words were beyond her, but she managed a nod. She did like it. A lot.

Gabe met her gaze with a smoldering look, his eyes blazing, his tone low and soothing and seductive. "Relax for me, sweetheart. I'm not going to do anything you don't want me to do."

Relaxing was the absolute last thing she could accomplish. Her thoughts swirled as he reached for the cream and squeezed a large dollop into his palm. She had no real idea what he intended, but the look on his face told her it would be sensual and that she'd probably enjoy it a great deal.

Should she allow this? How could she not allow it? Never in her entire life had a man pursued her. Certainly not a man like Gabe Kasper. She could do her thesis and indulge in an episode that might well prove to be the highlight of her entire life. Who was she kidding, she thought. It was already the highlight of her life!

She squeezed her eyes shut and held her breath, trying to order her thoughts, and suddenly felt his fingertips stroke up the inside of her thigh.

She moaned long and low, unable to quiet the sound. It came as much from expectation as from his touch.

"Look at me, Lizzy."

He was asking a lot, considered how tumultuous her emotions were at the moment. It took several seconds and the stillness of his hand on her leg for her to finally comply.

Gabe was breathing roughly. His mouth quirked the tiniest bit. "I don't know what it is about you, Red, but you make me feel like I'm going to explode." His fingers moved in a tantalizing little caress that made her breath catch. "Have you ever played baseball?"

She blinked, trying to comprehend the absurd question. "I...no."

Gabe nodded. "I'll teach you baseball. But probably not the kind of sport you think I mean." Still holding her gaze, he bent his golden blond head and pressed a soft, damp kiss onto her burned knee. "Much as I'd like to do otherwise, I think we'll just try first base tonight. If you don't like it, say stop and that'll be it. If you do like it, then tomorrow at the drive-in, we'll go to second base. Do you understand?"

He continued to place soft, warm kisses on her skin. Seeing his head there, against her legs, when no man had ever even gotten within touching distance before, was a fascinating discovery. She couldn't have conjured up something so hot, so erotic, in her wildest dreams.

"I think so." Her throat felt raw, but then she had an absolutely gorgeous hunk of a man kneeling at her feet, staring at her with lust, his hot fingers stroking her leg. "Is what you're doing now considered first base?"

Very slowly, Gabe shook his head. "No, this is just torture for me." He gave her a rascal's grin, and his blue eyes darkened. "For right now, I'm going to just finish putting on the cream. I want you as comfortable as possible. But to keep us both distracted, I'd like to learn a little more about you, okay?"

She probably would have agreed to anything in that moment. She was equally mesmerized and frantic and curious. "All right."

On his knees, Gabe opened his legs so that they enclosed her; his chest was even with her lap. He scooped more of the cream from his palm and began applying it in smooth, even strokes that felt like live fire. Not painfully, but with incredible promise.

"Tell me why you chose heroism for your thesis."

Oh, no. She couldn't explain that, not right now, not to him. She cleared her throat, trying to disassociate her mind from his touch so she could form coherent words. "I'm majoring in psychology. Most of the topics have been done to death. This seemed...unique."

Gabe tilted his head. "Is that right? What gave you the idea for heroism?"

She bit her lip, trying to sort out what she could tell him and what she couldn't. "I've always been fascinated by the stories of people who managed to muster incredible courage or strength at the time of need."

"Like the adrenaline rush? A woman who lifts a car to free her trapped child, a man who ignores burns to rescue his wife from a house fire. Those types of things?"

"Yes." The adrenaline rush that made saving someone important possible. Her throat tightened with the remembrance of how she'd failed, how she'd not been able to react at all, except as a coward.

"Hey?" Gabe finished her legs and carefully replaced the sheet, surprising her...disappointing her. "Are you all right, babe?"

His perceptiveness was frightening, especially when it involved a part of herself she fully intended to keep forever hidden. She went on the defensive without even stopping to think what she was doing or how he might view her response. Meeting his gaze, she said, "I'm not sure I like all these endearments you keep using. And especially not 'babe.' It sounds like you're talking to an infant."

Rather than hardening at her acerbic tone, his expression softened. "There's something you're not telling me, Lizzy."

Panic struck; she absolutely could not bear for him to nose into her private business. He was everything she wasn't, and she accepted that. But she didn't want her face rubbed in it. "I thought you were going to teach me about baseball!"

One side of his mouth kicked up, though his eyes continued to look shadowed with concern. "All right." He touched her chin with a fingertip. "Baseball is something we play in high school, but somehow I think you missed out on that."

His searching gaze forced her to acknowledge that with a nod. "I was very shy in high school."

"There was just you and your father, right?"

"Yes. But we were very close."

Gabe looked at her chest and she felt her breasts tighten in response. "That's good. But it can't make up for all the shenanigans and experiments and playfulness that teenagers indulge in with each other."

"My father," she admitted, willing to give him some truths, "tried to encourage me to go out more often. He was more than willing to supply me with the popular clothes and music and such. On my sixteenth birthday he even bought me a wonderful little car. But I wasn't really interested."

Talking was becoming more difficult by the moment. She knew Gabe was listening, but he was also caressing her with his eyes, and she knew what he saw. Her nipples were peaked, pressing against the white sheet almost painfully. But she liked the way he looked at her and didn't want him to stop.

With a bluntness that stunned her, Gabe suddenly said, "I'm going to touch your breasts. That's first base. All right?"

He didn't wait for her permission, but got more of the cooling cream and prepared to apply it her chest. Elizabeth held her breath, frozen, not daring to move for fear he'd stop—and for fear he wouldn't. She was excited, but also cautious. Whenever she'd imagined getting intimate with a man, she hadn't envisioned all this idle chitchat. She'd always assumed things would just...happen. She'd pictured getting carried away with passion, not having a man tease and explain and ask permission.

With the cream in one palm, Gabe closed his free hand around her wrist and gently pried her fingers from the sheet.

"Breathe, Lizzy."

She did, in a long choked gasp. The sheet slipped, but not far enough to bare her completely. Gabe's nostrils flared and his cheekbones flushed. He carried her shaking hand to his mouth and pressed a kiss into her palm, then placed her hand on her lap.

She tried to prepare herself but when she felt the cream on her skin she jumped. Again, Gabe whispered, "Shh..." in a way that sounded positively carnal. She was oblivious to the sting of her burned skin as his fingers dipped lower and lower. The edge of his thumb brushed her nipple.

His gaze leaped to hers, so intense she felt it clear to her bones. He leaned forward to blow on her skin. "I should be shot," he whispered, "for letting your sweet hide get burned like this."

His breath continued to drift over her, making gooseflesh rise, making her shiver in anticipation. His lips lightly touched the upper swell of her right breast. But that wasn't the only touch she was aware of. His hair, cool and so very soft, brushed against her and his hard muscled thighs caged her calves. Against one shin, she felt his throbbing erection.

She moaned.

Gabe nuzzled closer to her nipple, very close, but

not quite touching her there. "I like that, Lizzy, the way you make that soft, hungry little sound deep in your throat. It tells me so much."

His lips moved against her skin, adding to her sensitivity. She wasn't used to playing games, and she sure as certain wasn't used to wanting something so badly that her entire body trembled with the need. It wasn't a conscious decision on her part, but her hands lifted, sank into his hair and directed his mouth where she wanted it most.

Gabe gave his own earthy, raw groan just before his mouth clamped down on her throbbing nipple, suckling her through the sheet. Her body tensed, her back arching, her fingers clenching, her head falling back as her eyes closed. It was by far the most exquisite thing she had ever experienced. With her eyes closed, her senses were attuned to every rough flick of his tongue, the heat inside his mouth, the sharp edge of his teeth. She wanted to savor every sensation, store them all away to remember forever. Breathless, she whispered, "It's...it's not like I thought it'd be."

Gabe stroked with his tongue, soaking the sheet and plying her stiff nipple. "No?" His voice was a rough rasp and he sat back to view his handiwork, eyeing her shimmering breasts with satisfaction.

She didn't care. He could look all he wanted as long as he kissed her like that again. Shaking her head, Elizabeth ignored the way some of her hair tumbled free. "No," she admitted. "I used to daydream about a man doing that some day." She stroked his head, luxuriating in the cool silk of his thick hair. "But never a man like you, and it never felt quite that...deep."

His hands settled on either side of her hips, his long fingers curving to her buttocks. Heavy-lidded, he watched her. "What do you mean by deep?"

Elizabeth placed her hand low on her belly. "I feel it here. Every small lick or suck...I feel it inside me."

Gabe groaned again, then feasted on her other nipple. Elizabeth let her hands drift down his strong shoulders, then farther to his upper arms. She felt half insensate with the pleasure, half driven by curiosity to explore his pronounced biceps. His arms were rigid, braced hard on the chair and her behind.

He leaned back again, his breath heavy, his mouth wet. Still he looked at her body, not her face. "What did you mean, a man like me?"

Elizabeth had to gather her wits, had to force her eyes open. Gabe lifted one hand and, with the edge of his thumb, teased a wet nipple. The sheet offered no barrier at all, and when she looked down, Elizabeth could see that the sheet was all but transparent.

She wanted his mouth on her again.

"I always thought..." She swallowed hard, trying to form the correct words. "I'd hoped that some day I'd get intimate with a man, but I assumed he'd be more like me."

Slowly, Gabe's gaze lifted until he was studying her intently. But his hand was still on her breast, still driving her to distraction. "Like you, how?"

She shook her head. "Boring. Introverted. Something of a wallflower. Homely."

She gasped as Gabe lurched to his feet and glared

at her. Her mouth open in a small O, her eyes wide, she watched him, uncertain what had caused that sudden, heated reaction.

Gabe propped his hands on his lean hips, and his chest rose and fell with his labored efforts to gain control. His eyes were burning, his brows down, his mouth a hard line.

He shook his head and made a disgusted sound. "Damn it, Red, now you've gone and made me mad."

GABE WATCHED HER struggle to follow his words. She looked like sin and temptation and sweetness all wrapped together. Her heavy dark red hair was half up, half down, giving her a totally wanton look. Her skin was flushed beyond the sunburn, her eyes heavy lidded with sensuality but somewhat dazed by his annoyance.

It made him unreasonably angry for her to put herself down, though what she'd said had mirrored his earlier thoughts. Looking at her, he doubted any man could think her unattractive. He sure as hell didn't.

Reminded of that, he stalked a foot closer and grabbed her wrist, carrying her hand to his groin. Her mouth fell open as he forced her palm against his erection. "You know what that means, Red?"

She nodded dumbly, so still she wasn't even breathing.

"What? Tell me what it means?"

Her eyes left his face to stare at her hand, then to his face again. "That you're excited."

"Right. Do you think I'd get excited over a homely woman?"

She didn't answer.

He moved her hand, forcing her to stroke him, driving himself crazy. "The answer is no," he said with a rasp. "Now here's another question." The words were forced out through his teeth because Lizzy was no longer passive. Her hand had relaxed, opened, and her fingers curved around him. In a moment of wonder, Gabe realized he was the first guy she'd ever touched.

It was a heady thought.

He wasn't having an easy time controlling himself, but two deep breaths later, he finally managed to say, "Do you think, Red, that this happens to me often?"

"Yes."

That one breathy whispered word nearly made his knees buckle. He released her wrist and stepped back, but she leaned forward at the same time, maintaining the contact. "Well, you're wrong." He nearly strangled when she licked her lips in innocent, unthinking suggestion, her gaze still glued to his crotch. Gabe growled and said, "If you stroke me one more time you're going to see the consequences."

He clenched his fists, tightened his thighs, and luckily she let him go. When he could focus again, Gabe looked at her. Blinking rapidly, Lizzy continued to study his body. Suddenly aware of his renewed attention, she looked him in the eyes and asked, "Can I feel you some more?"

Yes. "No, not right now."

"When?"

He nearly choked on a laugh. "You persistent, curious little witch," he accused.

"You...you don't want me to?"

"I want you to too much."

Her tongue came out to stroke her lips again, making his blood thicken. "Then..."

"Tomorrow," he said quickly, before she could push him over the edge with her wanton questions. Knowing she wanted him, knowing he'd be the first man she'd ever explored, that she'd learn from him, was possibly the strongest aphrodisiac known to man. "At the drive-in. We'll go to second base, remember?"

Her eyes were dreamy. "You promise?"

Gabe gave one sharp nod while stifling a reflexive groan. He'd never survive. Was she wet right now? He'd be willing to bet she was, wet and hot, and he knew in every fiber of his being that she'd be so tight she'd kill him with pleasure. "I should go."

She came to her feet so fast she nearly stumbled over the sheet. Gabe caught her by the upper arms, heard her sharp intake of breath as his hands closed tightly on her burned skin, and he cursed himself. He released her, but she didn't step away; she stepped closer.

He felt like a total cad. "I can't believe I'm here seducing you when you're in pain." He'd aroused her, but there wasn't much chance of satisfying her without also causing her a lot of discomfort. She was so sunburned that just about any position would be impossible.

Her big eyes stared at him with wonder. "You were seducing me?"

Gabe stared at the ceiling, looking for inspiration

but finding none. "What the hell did you think I was doing, Lizzy?"

She said simply, "Playing with me."

"Oh, yeah." A fresh surge of blood rushed to his groin, making him break out in a sweat. He felt every pulse beat in his erection, and ground his teeth with the need to finish what he'd started.

He was so hard he hurt and he knew damn well he'd have a hell of a time sleeping tonight. "I'll play with you, all right. Playing with a woman's body is about the most pleasure a man can expect. And when a woman has a body like yours...I'm not sure I can live through it."

She stared at him while she chewed on her lips, and he could almost see the wheels turning. Gently, he touched a finger to her swollen mouth. "No, sweetheart, we can't tonight. You're in no shape to tussle with a man, and I'm too damn horny to be as careful as I'd need to be."

Her eyes flared over his blunt language, but he was too far gone to attempt romantic clichés. She touched his chest tentatively. "Would...would you like to just stay and talk for awhile?"

So you can work on seducing me? He knew he should say no, should remove himself from temptation, but he couldn't. She looked so hopeful, so sweet and aroused, he nodded. "Sure. Why don't you go get a dry sheet and I'll pour us some drinks. Sawyer did say you should have lots of fluids."

Her smile was beatific. "Okay."

Gabe watched the sassy sway of a perfect heart-shaped bottom and groaned anew. Damn, she was hot, and her being unaware of it only made her more so.

He found two tall glasses in the cabinet and opened the tiny apartment-size fridge. There was orange juice, milk and one cola. He poured two glasses of orange juice and carried them into the living room. When he set them down, he again noticed the pictures on the shelves and walked closer to examine them.

One was of a much younger Lizzy. Her red hair gave her away, although in the photo she wore long skinny braids and had braces on her teeth. Gabe grinned, thinking she looked oddly cute. An older woman with hair of a similar color, cut short and stylish, smiled into the camera while hugging Lizzy close. Her mother, Gabe decided, and felt a sadness for Lizzy's loss. No child should ever lose a mother at such a young age.

The other picture was of her father, sitting in a straight-backed chair, with Lizzy behind him. She had one pale hand on his shoulder; neither of them were smiling. Her father looked tired but kind, and Lizzy had an endearing expression of forbearance, as if she'd hated having the picture taken. She was older in this one, probably around seventeen. She was just starting to grow into her looks, he decided. Her freckles were more pronounced, her eyes too large, her chin too stubborn. Added years had softened her features and made them more feminine.

As Gabe went to replace the framed photograph on the shelf, he caught sight of an album. Curious, thinking to find more pictures of her and her life, Gabe picked it up and settled into the sofa. A folded transcript of her grades fell out. As he'd suspected, Lizzy was an overachiever, with near perfect marks in every subject. She'd already received recognition from the dean for being at the head of her class. He shook his head, wondering how anyone could take life so seriously. Then he opened the album.

What he found shocked him speechless.

There were numerous clipped articles, all of them focusing on her mother's death. They appeared to be from small hometown papers, and Gabe could relate because of all the fanfare he'd gotten in the local papers when he'd stopped the runaway boat.

Only these articles didn't appear to be very complimentary. Keeping one ear open for signs of Lizzy's return, Gabe began to read.

Girl fails to react: Eleanor Parks died in her car Saturday night after being forced off the road by a semi. The overturned car wasn't visible from the road, and while Elizabeth Parks escaped with nonfatal injuries, shock kept her from seeking help. Medical authorities speculate that, with timely intervention, Mrs. Parks may well have survived.

Appalled, Gabe read headline after headline, and with each word, a horrible ache expanded in his heart, making his chest too tight, his eyes damp. God, he could only imagine her torment.

Daughter Slow to React: Mother Dies
Unnecessary Death—The Trauma of Shock

Daughter Stricken with Grief—Must Be Hospi-
talized
Father Defends Daughter in Time of Grief

What could it have felt like for a twelve-year-old
child to accept the guilt of her mother's death? Not
only had she lost the one person she was likely closest
to, but she'd been blamed by insensitive reporters
and medical specialists.

Feeling a cross between numbness and unbearable
pain, Gabe carefully replaced the album beneath the
photos. He thrust his fisted hands into his pockets
and paced. So this was what had her in such an all-
fire tizzy to interview heroes. He grunted to himself,
fair sick of the damn word and its connotations. How
could an intelligent, independent woman compare
her reactions as a twelve-year-old child to those of a
grown man? It was ludicrous, and he wanted to both
shake her and cuddle her close, swearing that nothing would ever hurt her again.

He swallowed hard against the tumultuous, con-
flicting emotions that left him feeling adrift, uncertain
of himself and his purpose. When he heard her bedroom door open, he stepped away from the shelves
and crossed the carpeted floor to stare at her with vol-
atile feelings that simmered close to erupting. They
weren't exactly joyous feelings, but feelings of acute
awareness of her as a woman, him as a man, of the
differences in their lives and how shallow he'd been
in his assumptions.

Lizzy, wrapped in a very soft, pale blue terry-cloth

robe, widened her eyes at him and asked carefully, "Gabe? What's wrong?"

It felt like his damn heart was lodged in his throat, making it hard to swallow, doubly hard to speak. He hated it, hated himself and his cavalier attitude. Gently he cupped her face in his palms and bent to kiss her soft mouth, which still trembled slightly with the urges he'd deliberately created. He'd thought to say something soothing to her, something reassuring, but as her mouth opened and her hands sought his shoulders, Gabe decided on a different approach.

He'd get Lizzy over her ridiculous notions of guilt. He'd make her see herself as he saw her—a sexy, adorable woman filled with mysteries and depth. And he'd make damn sure she enjoyed herself in the bargain.

7

ELIZABETH FELT like she was floating, her feet never quite touching the ground. She said hello to the people she passed on the main street while heading to the diner to meet Misty and Honey Hudson. She hadn't had much sleep the night before, having been too tightly strung from wanting Gabe and from the slight lingering discomfort of her sunburn.

Today it was a toss-up as to which bothered her more. Gabe had stayed an additional hour, but he hadn't resumed the heated seduction. Instead, he'd been so painstakingly gentle, so filled with concern and comfort, it had been all she could do not to curl up on his lap and cuddle. He'd have let her. Heck, he'd tried several times to instigate just such a thing.

By the time he'd left and she'd prepared for bed, she'd been tingling all over, ultrasensitized by the brush of his mouth, the stroke of his fingertips, his low husky voice and constant string of compliments.

He thought her freckles were sexy. He thought her red hair was sexy. Oh, the things he'd said about her hair. She blushed again, remembering the way he'd looked at her while speculating on the contrast of her almost-brown brows and the vivid red of her hair, wondering about the curls on the rest of her body.

He was big and muscular and outrageous and all

male. She'd already decided that if he was willing to begin an involvement, she'd be an utter fool to rebuff him. The things he made her feel were too wonderful to ignore.

When she entered the small diner, several male heads turned her way. They didn't look at her as Gabe did, but rather with idle curiosity because she was a new face. She located the women, talking to a waitress at the back of the diner in a semiprivate booth. They all had their backs to her as she approached.

She was only a few feet away when she heard Misty say, "I think he's dumbstruck by his own interest. She's not at all the type of woman he usually goes after and he doesn't know what to make of that."

Honey laughed. "That's an understatement. Sawyer told me Gabe started chasing the ladies when he was just a kid, and he usually caught them. By the time he was fifteen, they were chasing *him*."

The waitress shook her head. Elizabeth recognized her as one of the women who'd been at the docks the day she'd first tracked down Gabe.

"That's nothing but the truth," the woman said. "Gabe can sit on the dock and the boats will pull in or idle by just to look at him. He always accepts it as his due, because it's what he's used to. I remember how he reacted when Elizabeth first showed up there. He didn't like her at all, but then she didn't seem to like him much, either, and I sorta think that's the draw. He's not used to women not gushing all over him."

"I just hope he doesn't hurt her. Gabe is a long way from being ready to settle down for more than a little recreation. But every woman he gets together with falls in love with him."

Misty agreed with her sister. "He's a hedonistic reprobate, but an adorable one."

Elizabeth was frozen to the spot. She wasn't an eavesdropper by nature, but she hadn't quite been able to announce herself. *In love with Gabe?* Yes, she supposed she was halfway there. How stupid of her, how naive to think he'd be truly interested in her for more than a quick tumble. As the women had implied, he evidently found her odd and was challenged by her.

The differences between her and Gabe had never felt more pronounced than at that precise moment. Because she was so inexperienced, not just sexually but when it came to relationships of any kind, she knew she'd be vulnerable to a man's attention. And Gabe wasn't just any man. His interest in her, no matter how short-term, was like the quintessential Cinderella story. Gabe was more than used to taking what he wanted from women, not in a selfish demand, but in shared pleasure. He'd assumed Elizabeth understood that, and that the enjoyment of playtime would be mutual. And it would be. She'd see to it.

A short, humorless laugh nearly choked her...and drew the three women's attention. Elizabeth mentally shook her head as she stepped forward with a feigned smile. None of it mattered; she still wanted him, wanted to experience everything he could show her, teach her. She wanted to really truly *feel* once again. Since her mother's death and the appearance of the harsh, dragging guilt, it seemed as if she hadn't really been living, that anything heartfelt or lasting had been blunted by the need to make amends, to understand her weakness.

Her heart hurt, but pride would keep her from showing it. She'd accept Gabriel Kasper on any terms, and he'd never know that she dreamed of more. She'd enjoy herself, without regrets, without demands.

Despite her past, she deserved that much.

The waitress, looking cautious, indicated a chair. "Hey, there, Elizabeth. Remember me?"

Again, Elizabeth smiled. "Ceily, from the boat docks, right? Yes, I remember. I hadn't realized you worked here." She carefully lowered herself into her seat and nodded at both sisters. Honey and Misty looked guilty, and Elizabeth tried to reassure them by pretending she hadn't heard a thing. "I hope I'm not too late?"

"Not at all," Misty said quickly. Her baby was sitting beside her in the booth on a pumpkin seat. "I hope you don't mind that I brought Amber along."

Elizabeth leaned over slightly to peer at the baby. "How could anyone ever object to that darling little angel?"

When she'd been a young girl, still fanciful and filled with daydreams, Elizabeth used to imagine someday having a baby, coddling it as her mother had coddled her, but she'd set those fantasies aside when she'd accepted her shortcomings.

Misty beamed at the compliment. "Strangely enough, she looks just like Morgan."

Ceily snorted at that outrageous comment. "Come on, Misty. I've never seen that little doll manage anything near the nasty scowl Morgan can dredge up without even trying."

Honey laughed. "That's true enough. But if Misty is even two minutes late to feed her, she has to contend with scowls and grumblings from both father and daughter. And I have to admit, they do resemble each other then. It sometimes seems to be a competition to see who can complain the loudest."

Misty slid a gentle finger over her sleeping daughter's cheek. "Morgan can't stand it if she even whimpers, much less gives a good howl. I swear, he shakes like a skinny Chihuahua if Amber gets the least upset."

Ceily made a sound of amused disgust. "I never thought I'd see the day when the brothers started settling down into blissful wedlock."

Honey nudged Elizabeth, then quipped in a stage whisper, "Not that Ceily's complaining. I think she's the only female in Buckhorn County who isn't pining for our men."

Being included in that "our men" category made Elizabeth blush, but no one noticed as Ceily broke loose with a raucous laugh. "I know the brothers far too well. We've been friends forever and that's not something I'd ever want to screw up by getting...romantic."

"A wise woman," Honey said, between sips of iced tea. "I think they all consider you something of a little sister."

Ceily bit her lip and mumbled under her breath, "I

wouldn't exactly say that." But Elizabeth appeared to be the only one who'd heard her.

Ceily took their orders and sauntered off. Elizabeth watched her surreptitiously, wondering just how involved the woman had been with the brothers. She was beautiful, in a very natural way, not bothering much with makeup or a fancy hairdo. She looked...earthy, with her light tan and sandy-brown hair. And Elizabeth remembered from seeing her in her bathing suit at the boat dock that Ceily was built very well, with the type of lush curves that would definitely attract the males.

She was frowning when Honey asked, "How's the sunburn?"

"Oh." Elizabeth drew herself together and shrugged. "Much better today. Your husband's cream worked wonders. Would you thank him again for me?"

Honey waved away her gratitude. "No problem. Sawyer is glad to do it, I'm sure."

Misty looked at her closely. "You don't look nearly as pink today. I guess it's fading fast."

Forcing a laugh, Elizabeth admitted, "I can even wear my bra today without cringing."

"Ouch." Misty looked appalled by that idea. "Are you sure you should? This blasted heat is oppressive."

It was only then that Elizabeth realized she was trussed up far more than Misty and Honey were. While they both wore comfortably loose T-shirts and cotton shorts with flip-flop sandals, Elizabeth had put a blouse under her long pullover dress and ankle socks with her shoes.

Deciding to be daring, she asked, "Does everyone dress so casually here? I mean, do you think anyone would notice if I wore something like that?" She indicated their clothes with a nod.

Honey laughed out loud. "Heck, yes. Gabe would notice! But then I get the feeling he'd notice you no matter what you wore. Watching him blunder around yesterday like a fish out of water was about the best entertainment we've had for awhile."

Misty bit her bottom lip, trying to stifle a laugh. "Gabe teased both Sawyer and Morgan something terrible when they got involved with us. Now he's just getting his due."

"But we're not involved." Even as she said it, Elizabeth felt her face heating. She hoped the sisters would attribute it to her sunburn and not embarrassment.

"Maybe not yet, but Gabe's working on it. I've gotten to know him pretty good since Sawyer and I married. He dates all the time, but he never mentions any particular woman. You he's mentioned several times."

Elizabeth didn't dare ask what he'd said. She could just imagine. "I think I'll buy myself some shorts today."

"Good idea. This is a vacation lake. Very few people bother to put on anything except casual clothes."

Ceily sidled up with Elizabeth's drink and everyone's food. Misty was having a huge hamburger with fries, but Honey and Elizabeth had settled on salads.

Misty made a face at them. "It's the breast-feeding, I swear. I never ate like a hog before, but now I stay hungry all the time. Sawyer says I'm burning off calories."

Honey pursed her lips, as if trying to keep something unsaid, then she appeared to burst. "I wonder if it'll affect me that way."

Misty froze with her mouth clamped around the fat burger. Like a sleepwalker she lowered the food and swallowed hard. "Are you...?"

Honey, practically shivering with excitement, nodded. Elizabeth almost jumped out of her seat when the two women squealed loudly and jumped up to hug across the table.

"When?" Misty demanded.

"In about six months. Late February." Honey leaned forward. "But keep it down. I don't want anyone else to know until I tell Sawyer."

"You haven't told him yet?"

"I just found out for sure this morning." She turned to Elizabeth. "We hadn't exactly been trying not to get pregnant, if you know what I mean, so it won't be a shock. But I still think he's going to make a big deal of it."

Wide-eyed, Elizabeth had no idea what to say to that. She was...stunned that the sisters had included her in such a personal, familial announcement. She'd never in her life had close female friends. She'd always been too odd, too alone, to mix in any of the small groups in school.

But as it turned out, Elizabeth didn't need to reply.

Honey and Misty went back to chattering while they ate, and Elizabeth was loath to interrupt.

Finally, they wore down and simply settled back in their seats, smiling. The silence wasn't an uncomfortable one, and Elizabeth found herself wondering about several things.

Trying to shake off her shyness, she asked, "Do you hope it's a boy or a girl?"

Honey touched her stomach with a mother's love. "It doesn't really matter to me. Amber is so precious—a girl would be nice. But then, Casey is such an outstanding young man that I think a son would be perfect, too."

Using that statement to lead into another question, Elizabeth pulled out her paper and pencil. "Do the brothers have any sisters?"

"Not a one. They only have male sperm, to hear them tell it." Misty had a soft, almost secret smile on her face. "Morgan calls Amber his little miracle."

Honey sighed. "Sawyer even warned me before we were married that I should resign myself to baby boys. The way they dote on Amber, as if none of them had ever seen a baby girl before, is hysterical. I keep telling them she's no different from Casey when he was an infant, but they just look at me like I'm nuts."

Elizabeth grinned at that image. "In a nice sort of way," she ventured cautiously, so she wouldn't offend, "they seem a bit sexist."

"Oh, they're sexist all right! And very old-fashioned, but as you said, in a nice way. They insist on helping a woman whenever they can, but they'd refuse to admit it if *they* needed help."

"Not that they ever do," Honey added. "They're the most self-reliant men I've ever seen. Their mother made sure they could cook and clean and fend for themselves."

Misty leaned forward to speak in a whisper. "Morgan says all he needs me for is to keep him happy." Her eyebrows bobbed. "You know what I mean." Then she settled back with a blissful sigh. "But then he'll show me it's so much more than that. We talk about everything and share everything. He unloads his worries at night over dinner and he says he misses me all day when he's working."

"Do you still work here in the diner?"

"Part-time, just for the fun of it. It keeps Morgan on his toes. He has this absurd notion that every guy in town comes here to eat just to ogle his wife." She laughed. "In truth, there's not a guy around who would look for more than two seconds for fear of incurring Morgan's wrath."

"He has a temper?"

"No, not really."

Honey choked, accidentally spraying iced tea across the table. Alarmed, Elizabeth quickly handed her a napkin. Biting back a laugh, Honey mumbled, "Sorry."

But Misty wasn't offended. "You should talk," she said primly. "Morgan is still bragging about that fight Sawyer had over you."

"What about Gabe?" Elizabeth asked. "Is he a hell-raiser?"

"Gabe? Heck, no, Gabe's a lover, not a fighter. Not

that I doubt he could handle himself in any situation."

Elizabeth tried to sound only mildly curious as she pursued that topic. "He has himself something of a reputation, doesn't he?"

Misty shrugged. "I suppose, but it's not a bad one. Folks around here just love him, that's all."

"You know," Elizabeth said thoughtfully as she set aside her pencil and propped her elbows on the table, "I think it's amazing that he did something so heroic and yet he shrugs it off as nothing."

Honey waved her fork dismissively. "They're all like that. They're strong and capable and well-respected and they don't really think a thing of it. To them, it's just how things are—they're nothing special. But I know not a one of them would sit on the sidelines if someone needed help. That's just the way they are."

For over an hour, the women talked, and Elizabeth took page after page of background notes on the brothers, Gabe specifically. If some of her questions had nothing to do with her thesis...well, that was no one's concern but her own.

When the lunch ended and she was ready to go, Elizabeth thanked both women. Misty had her wide-awake daughter cradled in her arms, cooing to her, so it was Honey who touched Elizabeth's arm and said, "I hope we've been some help."

Elizabeth could read the look in Honey's eyes and understood her meaning. She smiled in acknowledgment. "You don't have to worry. I know Gabe is still sowing his wild oats, so while I'm enjoying interviewing him, I'm not going to expect undying love. I'm a little more grounded in reality than that."

Honey bit her lip then shared a look with her sister. Misty sighed. "He really is a doll, isn't he?"

"Yes, he is. But he's a rascal too, and I'm well aware of just how serious he is, which isn't very. Besides, I'm only here for the summer. I have another semester of college to go and then job hunting before I can ever think of getting attached to anyone. Gabe is fun and exciting, but I know that's where it ends."

Misty slid out of the booth to stand before Elizabeth, her brow drawn into a thoughtful frown. "Now, I'm not sure you should rule everything out."

Honey agreed. "He is acting darned strange about all this."

"It doesn't matter." Elizabeth knew they wanted to be kind, to spare her. "I'm not letting anything or anyone get in the way of my goals."

"What are your goals? I know you said you're doing your thesis on the mystique of heroes, but why?"

"I'm hoping to go into counseling. Too often the ordinary person tries to compare herself to the true heroes of the world and only comes up lacking, which is damaging to self-esteem. I'd like to be able to prove that there are real, tangible differences to account for the heroes."

Before either sister could remark on that, Elizabeth asked for directions to Jordan's veterinary office. He was the only brother she hadn't spoken to yet. From what she'd heard, this particular brother was vastly different in many ways, but still enough to melt a woman's heart.

She looked forward to grilling him.

GABE WRAPPED HIS ARM around Ceily from behind, then gave her a loud smooch on her nape. "Hey, doll," he growled in a mock-hungry voice.

Jumping, Ceily almost dropped the tray of dirty dishes loading her down, and would have if Gabe hadn't caught it in time.

Rounding on him, Ceily yelled, "Don't do that, damn it! You about gave me a heart attack."

"Shh." Gabe grinned at her. "I don't want anyone to know I'm here."

Ceily seemed to think that was very funny, judging by her crooked grin. "If you're looking for your newest girlfriend, she already left."

Disappointment struck him, and he muttered a low curse that made Ceily's grin widen. "Do you know where she went?"

She took the tray from him and set it in the sink. "Maybe."

"Ceily..."

With a calculating look, she said over her shoulder, "I need a leaking faucet fixed. I can talk while you repair."

Gabe didn't want to waste that much time, but he reluctantly agreed. Ceily was one of his best friends, and she made one hell of a spy. Though she didn't gossip, she always seemed to know anything and everything that was said in her diner. "All right. Show me the sink."

Five minutes later Gabe was on his back, shirtless to keep from getting too dirty, trying to tighten a valve. The job was simple, but Ceily needed new plumbing in a bad way. "I can fix it for now, hon, but we're going to need to make major repairs soon. When's good for you?"

Ceily was at his side on a stool, taking a quick break while business was slow. "You just give me the word and I'll make the time."

Seconds later, Gabe shoved himself out from under the sink and sat up. "All done. So start talking."

Ceily checked the sink first, saw it was dry and nodded. "She went to see your brother Jordan, but she said she's also going to do some shopping." Ceily gave an impish smile. "She wants to dress more casual, like Misty and Honey."

Gabe groaned. Misty and Honey had chic comfort down to a fine art. The women could wear cutoffs and T-shirts and look like sex personified. "I'll never live through it."

Ceily thought that was about the funniest thing she'd ever heard. Gabe used her knee for unnecessary leverage and came to his feet. "You care to share the joke?"

"You don't think it's amusing that the mighty Gabe Kasper, womanizer and renowned playboy, is being struck down by a prim little red-haired wallflower?"

Anger tightened his gut for an instant before Gabe hid it. He didn't like anyone making fun of Lizzy, but he knew Ceily hadn't meant to be nasty. She, like him, was merely surprised at his interest in a woman who was so different from his usual girlfriends.

But then, that was precisely why he felt so drawn to her.

He began lathering his hands in the sink while he gathered his thoughts. Ceily tilted her head at his silence, then let out a whistle.

"Well, I'll be. You really are smitten, aren't you?"

"Smitten is a stupid word, Ceily," he groused. "Let's just call it intrigued, okay?"

"Intrigued, smitten...doesn't matter what you call it, Gabe, you've still got it bad." She crossed her arms and leaned against the wall. "Care to tell me why?"

Gabe lifted one shoulder in a shrug as he dried his hands on a frayed dish towel. "Lizzy is different."

"You're telling me!"

Gabe snapped her with the towel. "You *are* feeling sassy today, aren't you?"

She yelped, then rubbed her well-rounded hip. There was a time when Gabe would have helped her with that, but he had no real interest in touching any woman, even playfully, except Lizzy. She had invaded his brain, and it was taking a lot of getting used to.

Ceily was still frowning when she said, "It's not every day I get to witness the fall of the mighty Gabe."

Lifting one brow, Gabe announced, "I didn't fall, I jumped."

"So it's like that, huh?"

Gabe propped one hip on the side of the sink and watched Ceily. She was his friend and he'd always been able to talk with her. He loved his brothers dearly, but he could just imagine how they'd react if he started confessing to them. He'd never hear the end of it.

"It's damn strange," he admitted, "if you want the truth. One minute I didn't like her at all, then I was noticing all these little things about her, then I was lusting after her...."

"Uh, I hate to point this out, Gabe, but you tend to lust over every available, of-age woman you meet."

"Not like this." He shook his head and considered all the differences. "You know as well as I do that most of the women have come pretty easy for me."

Her look was ironic. "I have firsthand knowledge of that fact."

Gabe looked up, startled. A slow flush crept up his neck. "I wasn't talking about you, doll." He reached out and flicked a long finger over her soft cheek. "We were both too young then to even know what we were doing."

Ceily's smile was slow and taunting. Despite the fact they'd once experimented a little with each other, their friendship had grown. Gabe was eternally grateful for that.

"As I recall," she purred, teasing him, "you knew exactly what you were doing. And it was nice for my first time to be with someone I trusted and liked."

Gabe felt as though he was choking. Ceily hadn't mentioned that little episode in many years. And never would he point out to her exactly how inept he'd been back then. When she found the right guy, she'd realize it on her own. Curious, since she *had* brought it up, he asked, "Did you ever tell anyone?"

"Nope. And I know for a fact you haven't, so don't

get all flustered. Besides, I'm not carrying a torch for you, Gabe. It was fun, but I want more."

Gabe slid off the sink to give her a bear hug. Ceily was a very special person. "I know. And you'll find it. You deserve the very best."

She returned his hug and said with a hoity-toity accent, "I tend to think so." Then she shoved him back a bit. "But I know what you mean. All the women for miles around come running when you crook your little finger."

"Not all." Gabe almost chuckled at the image she described, but felt forced to admit the truth. "I have been turned down a time or two, you know."

Ceily scoffed. "Never with anyone who mattered."

Gabe stared at her, and her eyes widened. "Oh, wait! Are you telling me Elizabeth Parks turned you down?"

Scowling, Gabe shoved his hands in his pockets. "I'm not telling you anything about Elizabeth. My point was just that most women want me because of my reputation, because they think I'm good-looking or sexy—"

Ceily bent double laughing.

Gabe glared. "Oh, to hell with it. There's no talking to you today."

He started to skirt around her, but she caught him from behind and held on to his belt loops, getting dragged two feet before he finally stopped. Still chuckling, she gasped, "No, wait! I want to hear what it is that she wants from you."

Gabe heaved a deep sigh, then without turning to look at her, he admitted, "She thinks I'm some kind of damn hero and she wants to learn more about me, about my character and my family. She looks at me with this strange kind of excitement and...almost awe. Not for what *we* might do, or for what I might do to her, but for who she thinks I am. Damn, Ceily, no woman has ever done that before. And she hasn't pursued me at all for anything else. If I'd be willing to go on answering her damn questions, she'd be happy as a lark to leave it at that."

Last night, Gabe reminded himself, she'd been more than willing to do other things. But she hadn't come to him, he'd gone to her. He'd set about seducing her when he hadn't found it necessary to seduce a woman in ages.

And even then, he had the feeling that if he'd stuck her damn pencil in her hand, she'd have stopped cold in the middle of his sensual ministrations to start taking notes on his character. Now that he knew why it was so important to her, he not only felt turned on by her physically, he felt touched by her emotionally.

Seduction was a damn arousing business.

Ceily let go of his belt loops and smoothed her hand over the breadth of his back. "Poor Gabe. You really are adrift, huh?"

"I'm gonna turn you over my knee, Ceily."

She laughed at such a ridiculous threat. "No, you won't. Because I can give you some valuable advice."

Very slowly Gabe turned to face her. "Is that right?"

"Yep. You see, I heard Elizabeth tell your sisters-in-law that she has no intention of hanging around here once school starts. She's an academic sort and she has big plans for her life. If you hope to be part of those plans, you'd better get cracking, because I got the feeling that once she's gone, she won't be coming back."

8

WHEN GABE let himself in through the back entrance
of Jordan's veterinary clinic, he found Elizabeth and
Jordan leaning over an examination table. Their backs
were to him, but he could see that Lizzy was cuddled
close to Jordan's side, Jordan's arm was around her
shoulders, and they were in intimate conversation.

Gabe saw red.

"Am I interrupting?" He had meant to ask that
question with cold indifference, but even to his ears it
had sounded like a raw challenge.

Jordan looked at him over his shoulder; he was
smiling. "Come here, Gabe. Take a look." Then he
added, "But be very quiet."

His brother's voice had that peculiar soothing quality he used when treating frightened or injured animals. It was hypnotic and, according to all the
women, sexy as hell.

Gabe barely stifled a growl. If Jordan was using
that voice on Lizzy, he'd—

A very fat, bedraggled feline lay on the exam table,
licking a new batch of tiny mewling kittens. Gabe
glanced up at the look on Lizzy's face and promptly
melted.

Big tears glistened in her vivid blue eyes and
spiked her lashes. As Gabe watched, she gave a wa-

tery smile and sniffed, then gently rubbed the battered cat behind what was left of an ear.

Softly, Jordan explained, "She got into a tussle with a neighboring dog and lost. No sooner did she get dropped off than she started birthing. Eight kittens." Jordan shook his head. "She's a trooper, aren't you, old girl?" Jordan stroked his hand down the cat's back, earning a throaty purr.

Lizzy sniffed again. "She's a stray. Jordan says she's undernourished, so we didn't know if the kittens would be all right or not." She peered at Gabe with a worried expression. "They are awfully small, aren't they?"

Gabe smiled. "Most kittens are that tiny."

"And how...yucky they look?"

Jordan chuckled. "She'll have them all cleaned up and cozy in no time. The problem now is getting her into a pen. I hate to move her after she's just given birth, but I can hardly leave her and the babies here on the table."

Lizzy seemed to be considering that. "Do the pens open from the top or the front?"

"Both."

"Then... Well, maybe we could just take the table cover and all, and put her in the pen. I mean, if you hold the two top corners, and Gabe holds the two bottom corners, and I sort of guide it in and make sure no babies tumble out... Would that work do you think?"

To Gabe's annoyance, Jordan smiled and kissed Lizzy's cheek. "I think that's a brilliant idea. Gabe, keep an eye on this batch while I go find a big-enough pen. I'll be right back."

Gabe stepped next to Lizzy. "You've been crying." Just being close to her made him feel funny—adrift, as Ceily had said. He didn't know himself when he was this close to her, and he sure as hell didn't recognize all the things she made him feel.

Lizzy bit her lip, which looked extremely provocative to Gabe. "I've never seen babies born before. It's amazing."

Gabe slipped his arm around her and nuzzled her ear. Keeping his hands, or his mouth, to himself was out of the question. "Did you help Jordan?"

She laughed softly. "Mostly I just tried to stay out of his way."

Jordan said from behind them, "I couldn't have done it without her. She has the touch, Gabe. No sooner did she stroke that old cat than she settled down and relaxed some. I was afraid I was going to have to sedate her, but Elizabeth's touch was better than any shot I could give."

Gabe made a noncommittal sound. He knew firsthand just how special Lizzy's touch was.

Within minutes they had the mother and all her babies cozied up in the pen and set in a warm corner where there was plenty of sunshine and quiet. The mother cat, exhausted after her ordeal, dozed off.

"Will she be all right?" Gabe asked.

Elizabeth answered him. "Jordan said none of her injuries from the dog are significant. He cleaned up some scrapes and scratches, one not too horrible bite, and then she started birthing." Laughing at herself, Lizzy admitted, "When she let out that first screeching roar, I thought she was dying. Jordan explained to me that she was just a mama in labor."

Jordan, trying to slip clean dry bedding in around the mewling kittens, said, "Gabe, why don't you show Elizabeth around the rest of the clinic?"

Lizzy's eyes widened. "Could you? I'd love to see it."

Since Gabe would love to get her alone, he agreed.

Everything about Elizabeth Parks fascinated him— her softness, her freckles, her temper, her awe at the sight of a yapping puppy or a sleeping bird. She was complex in many ways, crystal clear in others. By the time they were done looking around, Jordan had finished with the kittens and he showed no hesitation in embracing Lizzy again.

Gabe wanted to flatten him.

"Come back any time, Elizabeth." He glanced at Gabe. "We can talk more."

"I'd like that. Thank you."

Gabe knew his ears were turning red, but damn it, he didn't want her hanging around Jordan. He didn't want her hanging around any man except himself.

And he still wasn't too keen on her discussing him with everyone. God only knew what she might hear!

She finally stepped away from Jordan and faced both men. "I have to run off now. I have more errands to get through."

She backed to the door as she said it, keeping a close watch on Gabe.

"What errands?" he asked suspiciously.

"Oh, the usual." She reached for the doorknob and

opened the door. "The library, the grocery store...a visit with Casey."

The last was muttered and it took a second for it to sink in. Gabe scowled and started toward her. "Now wait just a damn minute—"

"Sorry! Gotta go." She hesitated, then called, "I'll see you tonight, Gabe!"

She was out the door before he could catch her. He would have given pursuit if Jordan hadn't started laughing. At that moment, Gabe's frustration level tipped the scales and he decided Jordan would make a fine target. Slowly he turned, his nostrils flared. "You have something to say?"

Jordan was his quietest brother, but also the deepest. He kept his thoughts to himself for the most part, and tended to view the world differently than the rest of them. He was more serious, more sensitive. Women loved him for those qualities.

What had Elizabeth thought of him?

Gabe waited and finally Jordan managed to wipe the grin off his face. "I'd say Elizabeth Parks is pretty special."

Gabe's muscles tightened until they almost cramped. He hadn't thought her special at first, but now that he did, he didn't want anyone else—anyone male—to think it. "Me, too," he snarled.

Jordan was supremely unaffected by his anger. "Going to do anything about it?"

"It?"

Jordan shook his head as if he pitied Gabe. "You remind me of a junkyard dog who's just sniffed a female in heat. You're trying to guard the junkyard and still lay claim to the female."

"I'm not at all sure I like that analogy."

Jordan shrugged. "It fits. And if I was you, I'd get my head clear real quick."

Because he wasn't sure how to do that, Gabe didn't comment. Instead, he asked, "What did you think of her?"

"Sexy."

That single word hit him like a solid punch in the ribs. He wheezed. "Damn it, Jordan..."

"What? You think you're the only one to notice?" Again, Jordan shook his head. "I've got a waiting room full of clients, so I'll make this quick. No, Elizabeth's sex appeal isn't up-front and in your face. But it only takes about two minutes of talking with her, of watching her move and hearing her voice and looking into those incredible blue eyes to know she's hotter than hell on the inside."

It was so unlike Jordan to speak that way that Gabe was rendered mute.

"If you could have seen how gentle her hands were when she touched that frightened cat, well... You can imagine where a man's mind wanders when seeing that. And the look of discovery on her face when the first kitten appeared, and her husky voice when she's getting emotional..." Jordan shrugged. "It doesn't take a rocket scientist to know those same qualities would carry over into the rest of her life. She's sensitive and tenderhearted and something about her is a little wounded, making her sympathetic to boot."

Gabe rubbed both hands over his face, those elusive emotions rising to choke him.

Jordan slapped him on the back. "Add to that an incredible body... Well, there you have it."

"I'm sorry I asked," Gabe moaned.

Jordan turned his brother around and steered him toward the door. They were of a similar height and build, but Gabe was numb, so moving him was no problem. "Go. I have work to do."

Gabe was just over the threshold when Jordan said his name again. Turning, Gabe raised one brow.

"I talked you up real nice, told her what a sterling character you have, but somehow I got the impression she's given up on you already." Jordan shrugged. "Not that she isn't interested, because I could tell she is. I'm not sure what you've been doing with her, and it's certainly none of my business, but every time she said your name, she blushed real cute."

Eyes narrowed, Gabe muttered, "That's sunburn."

"No, that was arousal. Credit me with enough sense to know the difference."

Gabe started back in and Jordan flattened a hand on his sternum, holding him off. "The thing is," Jordan said with quiet emphasis, "her thoughts are as clear as the written word, and from what I could tell, she's determined that what she feels is only sexual. So if that's not what you want, I'd say you have a problem. One that you better start working on real quick."

It was the second time in one day that Gabe had been given that advice. Without another word he stomped off, his mind churning with confusion. Yes, he wanted more, but how much more? Hell, he barely knew the woman. And she did have an education to finish, one that was obviously important to her.

All he could do, Gabe decided, was take it day by day. He'd get inside her brick wall, get her to talk to him, and maybe, with any luck, he'd find out that Elizabeth wanted him for more than a sexual fling or a college thesis.

But for how much more was anyone's guess.

ELIZABETH FELT like a puddle of nerves on the drive to the movies that night. In quite a daring move, she'd changed from her earlier clothes into another dress, this one a tad shorter, landing just below her knees, and with a bodice that unbuttoned. She felt downright wanton. Not because the clothing was in any way revealing, but because of why she'd chosen it in the first place.

Thinking of Gabe's hands stealing under her skirt in search of second base or opening her buttons to linger on first base had her in a frenzy of anticipation.

Nervously, she glanced at his profile. He was quiet, his jaw set as he concentrated on driving. His strange, introspective mood seemed to permeate the car. She cleared her throat and said boldly, "Do you realize how many firsts I've had since meeting you?"

He jerked, his gaze swinging toward her for a brief instant. "What's that supposed to mean?"

She had to make him understand, Elizabeth thought. The last thing she wanted to happen, now that she was getting into the novelty of this unique courtship, was for Gabe to feel pressured and back off. His sisters-in-law had been clearly concerned that she might get hurt. Perhaps Gabe would worry about the same thing. But if she reassured him that they wanted the same thing, a pleasant way to pass the time during her visit, with no strings attached, then he'd feel free to continue his wonderful attentions.

And they were wonderful. Gabe made her feel sexy, when all her life she'd felt plain to the point of being invisible. He made her feel feminine when she'd never paid much attention to her softness before, except that it made her weaker, less competent in a crisis. And he made her feel sexually hungry when she hadn't even known such a hunger existed.

"I like your brother."

Gabe shot her a dark look. "Which one?"

"Well, all of them, but I was talking about Jordan. He's different from the rest of you."

Gabe's hands squeezed the wheel tightly. "Yeah? How so?"

"Quieter. More...intense. He's so gentle with the animals. I felt totally at ease with him, and that was certainly a first."

Gabe's jaw locked so hard she wondered that he didn't get a headache. "You're not at ease with me?"

Around Gabe she was tense and so hot she thought she might catch fire. But she wouldn't tell him that. "It was just different with Jordan. And he let me help with that cat. I've never seen babies born before." Her voice softened, but she couldn't help it. Seeing the tiny little wet creatures emerging was a true miracle. "Have you? Seen babies born, I mean?"

"Sure." Gabe glanced at her, then at the road. "Jordan keeps all kinds of pets around the house. We all like animals, Lizzy. He's not different in that."

"But Jordan's... I don't know. More discreet than the rest of you. Softer."

"Ha!" Gabe shifted in his seat, looking disgruntled. "Don't let Jordan fool you! He's quieter, I'll give you that. But he's a man, same as I am."

"Gabe, I didn't mean to draw a comparison." She couldn't understand his reaction. It was almost as if...no. There was no way Gabriel Kasper could be jealous of his brother. She decided to change the subject.

"I had lunch with Honey and Misty today."

Gabe's brows pulled down the tiniest bit. "Did you enjoy yourself?"

"Yes." Elizabeth pleated the edge of her skirt with her fingertips. "I've never really hung out with other women before. It was fun. The things they talk about..."

There was a strange darkness to his eyes as he asked, "What things?"

She shrugged. "Women things." She had no intention of telling him Honey was pregnant. Now that she'd been initiated into the wonders of doing lunch with the ladies, she'd didn't want to do anything to ruin it. When Honey told her husband the news, then Gabe would find out. "Shopping, Amber, men. Things like that."

In a reflexive movement, Gabe's hands tightened on the steering wheel. "What about men?"

"Nothing in particular. Just fun stuff. It was a first for me. I hadn't realized how enjoyable that could be, chatting and laughing with other women. I've never quite fit in like that before, but they're so nice and accepting. I like your sisters-in-law."

Gabe stopped for a red light and turned to face her. "I like them, too. A lot." He tilted his head, studying her, and there was something in his eyes, some vague shadow of consideration. "C'mere, Lizzy."

Oh, the way he said that. It was so much more than an invitation to close the space between them. The heat in his eyes made it more. The low growl of his voice made it more. She looked at the seat where Gabe's large hand rested. Warming inside, she scooted over as much as her seat belt would allow. It was close enough to feel his heat, his energy, to breathe in his wonderfully musky male scent.

Last night she had imagined burying her nose against his neck, drinking him in and tasting his hot skin with her tongue.... She gulped a large breath of air and tried to get control of herself. She was turning into a nymphomaniac!

Immediately, Gabe's rough palm settled on her thigh in a possessive hold that thrilled her.

"How's your sunburn today?" he murmured, gently caressing her.

Staring at his dark hand on her leg, she shrugged. "Much better. It was a little tender this morning, but now I hardly notice it at all."

He slipped his fingers beneath the skirt of her dress and began tracing slow, easy circles on her flesh. Her breathing deepened. "And this? Does this hurt you, Lizzy?"

She shook her head, too startled, too excited to speak.

The light turned green and Gabe pulled away. He used one hand to steer while his gentle fingers continued to pet her bare skin. "Tell me what other firsts we're talking about."

His warm touch was hypnotic and she found her legs parting just a bit so his searching fingers could drift lazily up the sensitive inside of her knee. "Swimming in a lake."

"Oh, yeah." He flashed her a grin. "Think you might want to be daring and try it again sometime?"

This must be old hat to him, Elizabeth thought, as he easily maneuvered the car one-handed while deliberately arousing her with the other. He was such a rogue.

"Yes." She'd try anything Gabe wanted her to. She trusted him.

"Any other firsts?"

"Well, there's...this." She indicated his hand beneath her skirt, slowly inching higher. She sucked in air and concentrated on speaking coherently. "The kissing and touching and the way you...talk to me."

He glanced at her and she said, "I love the way you talk to me, Gabe. No man has ever spoken so intimately with me, much less said the kinds of things you say."

"You've known a lot of fools, sweetheart."

Her smile trembled. "There, you see? And all this business with first base and drive-in movies. I feel like I'm just starting to really see the world."

Gabe squeezed his eyes closed for a heartbeat, and

she added, "You're also by far the most unique hero I've interviewed, so I suppose that's a first, as well."

How in the world she'd managed to string so many words together, she had no idea. Her thoughts felt jumbled, her nerve endings raw. Leaning slightly toward him, she touched his shoulder. "Gabe, can I ask you something?"

Twilight was settling in on the small town, making it almost dark enough to hide what they did with each other. Elizabeth smoothed her hand over his shoulder, then down to squeeze his biceps. She soaked in the feel of the soft cotton T-shirt over solid muscle. Gabe felt so good.

He worked his jaw. "You can ask me anything, babe."

Hesitantly, she explained, "It's sort of a request."

His hand left her as he pulled into a gravel lot behind several other cars, waiting to pay at the drive-in entrance. Elizabeth looked around in wonder. People milled about everywhere, some walking to a concrete-block building that she assumed housed the cameras and perhaps a concession stand. Others leaned in car windows talking to neighbors. Some were sitting outside their cars or trucks or vans, watching the sky darken and the stars appear. The screen was huge, situated in front of row after row of metal poles holding speakers. It fascinated her.

"Ask away."

"Oh." Turning to Gabe, she bit her bottom lip, then because she was unable to look at him and ask her question, she gave her attention to the surrounding lot. "Would it be okay if I touched you, too? I mean, like with first base and second base? Touching you last night…that was another first. I had no idea a man felt so…contradictory."

His Adam's apple bobbed when he swallowed hard. He adjusted his jeans, slouched behind the wheel a bit more and closed his eyes. "Contradictory, how?"

Elizabeth knew her face was flaming. Actually, her whole body was flaming. In a rough, strangled whisper, she said, "Soft in some places, so hard in others. Sleek and alive. I'd…I'd like to feel your chest, under your shirt, and I'd like to feel you…*there*, inside your jeans."

Gabe groaned, then laughed. He rested his forehead against the steering wheel for one second, then swiveled to snare her with his gaze. "Are you absolutely sure you want to see a movie?"

Not quite understanding, Elizabeth glanced at the billboard announcing which titles would be playing tonight. The first movie was *Tonya's Revenge*. Probably an action movie, she decided—not her favorite. But while it didn't sound exactly scintillating, she was very curious. "I'd like to see at least a bit of it, since this is another first for me. Why?"

Gabe hesitated to answer as he pulled up to the small cashier's window and handed over a couple of bills. The attendant, evidently someone Gabe knew based on his greeting and his curiosity as he speared a flashlight into the car to check out Elizabeth, winked and handed Gabe his change. "Enjoy the movie," he said with a wide grin. Gabe answered with a muttered oath.

Elizabeth looked around as Gabe parked the car toward the back of the lot. Already people had set up lawn chairs and blankets or turned their trucks around to relax in the truck beds. Gabe moved as far away from the others as he could.

"You don't want to stay, do you?" Elizabeth didn't want to force him into something he was reluctant to do.

Gabe's frown became more pronounced. "I'm having second thoughts, that's all."

Her stomach pitched in very real dread. "Second thoughts? You mean you don't want to—"

In a sudden move, Gabe grabbed her by the back of the neck and hauled her close, then treated her to a hot, deep, tongue-licking kiss that left her shaken. With his mouth still touching hers, he said, "I want," he assured her in a low growl. "But I'd rather be back at your apartment where I could get you naked and feast on you in private."

Elizabeth could barely get her heavy eyelids to open. Her heart felt ready to burst, her skin too tight, her breasts and belly too sensitive. Breathless, she asked, "And you'd let me touch you, too?"

"Hell, yeah." He kissed her again, short and sweet. "But I don't want you to miss any firsts here, sugar. And every American woman should experience the drive-in at least once. Better late than never, I suppose."

Elizabeth nuzzled his warm throat, just as she'd imagined doing. She luxuriated in his exotic, enticing scent. What would it be like to have that scent surrounding her all night long? Trying to follow the conversation, she asked, "Because the movies are good?"

Gabe grinned, but it was a carnal grin, filled with determination and sultry heat. "No, baby." He held her a little closer, his hand splayed on the small of her back. "It's because getting groped at the drive-in is practically a tradition. You can't really be at the movies without doing at least a little petting. The lights are dim, the movie's boring and all that body heat builds up. It's just natural to get a little frisky."

Elizabeth considered that, then slowly slid both hands up Gabe's chest to his shoulders, then around his neck. "How about if I want to do a lot of petting?"

"Then I'll maybe last through half a movie. *Maybe.*" He cradled her head between his hands and rubbed her cheekbones with his thumbs. "But I'm not making any promises, sweetheart, so don't say I didn't warn you."

9

SHE WAS DRIVING him crazy. Lizzy's sweet, hot mouth opened on his throat and she made a nearly incoherent sound of discovery and excitement. "You taste so good, Gabe. Do you taste the same all over?"

Feeling her soft lips move against his skin, he tightened painfully from toes to scalp. He wanted to let her explore, to take her time and experience everything, but he wasn't sure he'd live through it. "You can find out later," he murmured, and just saying the words almost sent him off the deep end while images of her mouth on his abdomen, his thighs, in between, fired him. He groaned.

She leaned back slightly and looked at the movie. "What?"

There was a breathless excitement to her tone as she anticipated another love scene on the big screen. He'd had no idea Lizzy would be so receptive to the somewhat cheesy, low-grade erotic film that was playing. Watching her while she watched the movie, he wedged his palm beneath her breast and felt the frantic racing of her heartbeat.

She amused him. And fascinated him. Grinning, he teased, "Lizzy. I'm surprised you can even see the movie the way we've steamed up the windows."

Her smile was pleased and filled with feminine

power. "I'd read about fogging windows in books before, but I thought it was an exaggeration."

Forget amusement. Her naïveté made him rock hard with lust and soft as butter with affection. Bringing her mouth to his, he said against her lips, "Just looking at you is enough to steam the place up," then proceeded to thoroughly feast on her mouth. He'd never tire of her taste, her warmth. The small, sexy sounds she made when he gave her his tongue, or when he coaxed her tongue into his mouth.

She grew quickly impatient with kissing and started tugging on his T-shirt, untucking it from his jeans.

Gabe, always willing to oblige, set her a bit away from him and pulled it over his head. Within a heartbeat she was back, her eyes luminous in the dark interior of the car, her small hands eagerly sliding over his hot skin. Whether on purpose or not, he didn't know, her thumbs brushed over his nipples and he jerked. She stared, wide-eyed, at his reaction, made a sound of discovery and deliberately delved her hands into the hair on his chest again.

"Sweet mercy..." Gabe groaned, knotting his hands against the seat and dredging up thoughts of work, of the lake, anything to try to regain some measure of control.

Then her mouth touched his right nipple and he felt her gentle, moist breath, the tentative flick of her small pink tongue...and he was gone.

"Sorry," he rasped. "I can't take it." He saw the disappointment in her gaze and choked on a strangled breath. Holding her slim shoulders to keep her at bay, he said, "Not here, sweetheart. It's just too much. You're too much. I don't understand it, but..."

She didn't look convinced, so he caught her hand and carried it to his erection, then hissed a painful breath as the contact made his entire body clench.

"You see what you're doing to me?" he asked. He knew his voice was harsh, guttural, knew he'd started to sweat and that his hands were shaking. "It's insane. I've made out in this drive-in hundreds of times, but I've never been this close to losing all reason."

"Really?"

He blinked at her look of wonder, minutely regaining his wits. She honestly had no idea of her appeal or her effect on the male species. "Yeah. I'm sorry, babe, but it's the truth." For the first time in his life, his salacious past embarrassed him a bit. Lizzy was so innocent, so pure, that he felt like a total scoundrel. "My mother should have locked me up or something," he muttered, his long fingers still encircling her wrist, holding her hand immobile against him. "Sawyer told her to often enough. Morgan even tried it a few times. But I was always more wild than not and I was determined to get my fill and..."

He trailed off as he realized how fascinated she was, soaking up his every absurd word. Good God, he hoped she didn't put any of that in her damn thesis!

Shaking her gently, he added, "Lizzy, listen to me. There's something about you...."

She tilted her head at him in a measure of pity. "What? My freckles? Come on, Gabe. I've never heard of freckles inspiring lust. Or red hair that's too curly. Or..."

Gabe curved his hand around one lush breast. He could feel the warmth and softness of her, the incredible firmness of virgin flesh. "How about a body made for a man?" he growled. "Or a smile that's so sweet I feel it inside my pants."

She gasped.

"Or skin so soft it makes me crazy wanting to feel it all over my body. Or the way you talk, the things you talk about, your innocence and your daring and your—"

She pressed her fingers over his mouth, her eyes squeezed shut. He parted his lips and ran the tip of his tongue down the seam of her middle and ring finger, probing lightly. She snatched her hand away and panted.

"I want you, Lizzy."

Her eyes opened slowly and they glowed. "I want you, too." She gulped in air, then added, "Just for the summer, for this one time in my life, I want to experience everything I've never felt before. When I go back to school and my old life-style and my plans, when I start my formal training, I want it to be with new knowledge. I don't want to be inexperienced anymore. I want to loosen up, as you suggested."

Gabe took her words like an iron punch on the chin. *Just for the summer, just for the summer...*

Damn her, no! He wouldn't give up that easy. But he also didn't want to scare her off. He'd give her everything she asked for and more. He'd drown her in pleasure so intense she'd get addicted. She wouldn't be able to do without him. He'd tie her so closely to him she wouldn't even be able to think about walking away from him.

He had no idea what the murky future held, but for the first time in his life he was anxious about it. A year from now? Who the hell knew? Lasting romantic relationships weren't his forté, but he'd seen his two oldest brothers work it out, and that was nothing short of a miracle. One thing he was certain about: a month from now he'd still be wanting her, today, tomorrow...maybe indefinitely. He wanted, he *needed*, a chance to see what was happening between them.

Gabe reached to the floor of the car and picked up the box of popcorn they'd bought earlier. He put it in her lap. "Hold onto that."

"Gabe?"

He didn't look at her again as he stuck the speaker out the window and hooked it into place on its stand. A lot of people would recognize his car, and they'd know he was leaving early. They'd probably even deduce why. For Lizzy's sake, he hated that, but couldn't think of an alternative. It would be worse if he ended up doing things with her here that he knew damn good and well should be done in private. And his control was too strained. Already he wanted her so bad he felt sweat forming on his naked back and at his temples, though the night had cooled off and was comfortable.

Even without the speaker in the car, he heard the on-screen moaning and looked up. *Tanya's Revenge* wasn't much in the way of evil intent. Gabe figured she planned to physically, sexually wear out her adversary, then gain her revenge—whatever it might be. Lizzy was spellbound. She'd watched every sex scene with single-minded intent.

His heart pounded in his chest as he considered doing all those things to her, and how she would react. "Put your seat belt back on."

Without tearing her gaze from the screen, she obeyed. His car started with a low purr and then they were maneuvering out of the lot. Once the screen was no longer in view, Lizzy turned toward him. He could feel her curiosity, could almost hear her mind working, thinking about what she'd watched and wondering if they'd do things like that together.

"Damn right we will," Gabe said, answering her silent question. Lizzy fanned herself, but otherwise held quiet. They reached her place in record time. In one minute flat they were inside with the door locked and Gabe had her pressed to the wall, giving his hands and his mouth free rein.

ELIZABETH held her breath as Gabe's right hand stroked down her side, over her waist, her hip, then to the back of her knee. He pulled her leg upward so that she was practically circling his hips—then he thrust gently.

A moan escaped her. She could feel the fullness and hard length of his erection through his jeans as he deliberately rocked against her in a parody of sex. His mouth, open and damp, moved over her cheek to her arched throat. "I want to be inside you right now, babe. I *need* to be inside you."

"My...my bedroom," she muttered, nearly incoherent, more than ready to accommodate him. But Gabe shook his head.

"You have to do some catching up. I want you to be as hot as I am."

She tried to tell him that she already was, but then his mouth covered hers and his tongue licked past her lips and she could barely think, much less speak.

His hand, rough and incredibly hot, smoothed over her bare thigh to her panties. Elizabeth couldn't stop her instinctive reaction to his hand on her bottom, exploring, first palming one round cheek then gliding inward to touch her in the most intimate spot imaginable.

"Easy," he whispered against her mouth. "Damn, you're wet. You do want me, don't you, sweetheart?"

"Yes..." She felt like she was falling, though her back was flat against the wall with Gabe's hard torso pinning her in place.

"Let's get these out of the way." He released her leg and hooked both hands into the waistband of her panties beneath her skirt. It felt naughty and exciting and achingly sexual the way he went to one knee in front of her to strip off her underclothes. "Step out of them," he instructed.

Like a sleepwalker, Elizabeth lifted first one foot and then the other. Her sandals were still in place, but Gabe had no problem tugging her panties off around them. She waited for him to stand, but he didn't, and she looked down.

His face was flushed, his eyes burning hot as he kneaded the backs of her thighs. He looked at her and didn't smile. Instead he leaned forward and kissed her through her cotton dress, making her suck in a startled, choking breath. Her hands automatically sought his head and her fingers threaded into his cool blond hair.

"Gabe?"

"You smell good," he said, nuzzling into her. Her knees threatened to give out, but his palms moved to cuddle her naked backside, keeping her upright. "So good."

"I...I can't do this." Even as she said it, her hands clenched in his hair, directing his attentions to a spot that pulsed with need. His mouth opened and his breath was incredibly hot, almost unbearable. She felt the damp press of his tongue through her clothes and she cried out.

Gabe shot to his feet in front of her and took her mouth in a voracious kiss meant to consume her. She couldn't breathe, couldn't react, couldn't think. She felt wild, this time lifting her leg to wrap around him without instruction. Both his hands covered her breasts, squeezing a bit roughly, but she loved it, loved him and the way he made her feel.

He started on the buttons of her dress and had them all free within seconds. The bodice opened just wide enough for him to tug it down her shoulders and beneath her breasts. The dress framed her, caught at her elbows and pinning her arms to her sides. "Gabe?" She struggled, wanting to touch him, too.

The dress pulled taut and forced her straining breasts higher. Her nipples were stiff, pointed, and with a low growl Gabe bent and sucked one deep into the heat of his mouth, his rough tongue rasping over her, his teeth holding her captive for the assault.

She screamed. Her body arched hard against his. Gabe switched to the other nipple and his hands went under her skirt, one lifting her thigh, the other cupping over her belly then delving into her moist curls. She knew she was wet, could feel the pulsing of her body. His fingers were both a relief and a torture as he moved them over her hot flesh, stroking, then parting slick, swollen folds.

She pressed her head against the wall, feeling a strange tension begin to invade her body.

"We'll go easy," he promised, but the words were so low, so rough, she could barely understand them. "Right here, sweetheart," he murmured, and she felt a lightning stroke of sensation as one fingertip deliberately plied her swollen clitoris. Gasping, she tried to pull away because the sensation was too acute, but there was no place for her to go.

"Don't fight me," he whispered around her wet nipple, licking lazily. "Trust me, Lizzy."

She couldn't. The feelings were coming too fast, too strong. Her muscles ached and tightened, then tightened some more. Her vision blurred as heat washed over her in waves. She tried to tell him it was too much, but her words didn't make any sense and he ignored them anyway, listening more to her body than what she had to say. His fingertip felt both rough and gentle as he continued to pet her, concentrating patiently on that one ultrasensitive spot, driving her insane.

Her climax took her by surprise, stealing her

breath, making it impossible to do more than moan in low gasping pants, going on and on.... Her body bowed, but Gabe held her securely, not stopping his touch, pushing her and pushing her. He moaned, too, the sound a small vibration around her nipple as he sucked strongly at her. His left forearm slipped beneath her buttocks, keeping her on her feet as her knees weakened, forcing her to feel everything he wanted her to feel.

When finally she slumped against him, spent and exhausted, his hold gentled, loosened. She was no longer crushed against his body, but remained in his embrace, gently rocking. His palm cupped her, holding in the heat, and he said, "I can still feel you pulsing."

Embarrassment tried to ebb into her consciousness, but Gabe didn't give it a chance to take hold. He kissed each breast, her throat, her chin. Putting his forehead to hers, their noses touching, he whispered, "That was incredible, Lizzy."

If she'd had the strength she would have laughed. Gabe was a master of understatement. Slowly she opened her eyes and was seared by the heat in his. While she watched, he removed his palm from her and raised his hand to her face. His gaze dropped to her mouth and with one wet fingertip, he traced her lips.

She sucked in a startled breath, but couldn't think of a thing to say. Still watching her, Gabe slowly licked her upper lip, then pulled her bottom lip through his teeth to suck gently. "You taste as sweet as I knew you would."

She couldn't move. Her eyes opened owlishly. Good grief, she'd never been in this situation before, never even imagined such a thing! He hadn't shared intercourse with her, but she supposed this was one form of lovemaking. Only...against her front door? With her panties off and his clothes still on and his magical fingers...

"Cat got your tongue?" he asked while smoothing her hair from her face.

"I..." She swallowed hard. "I don't know what to say."

"How about, 'Gabe I want you.'" His gaze moved over her face in loving detail, his fingers gentle on her temple. She noticed his hands shook.

"Gabe, I want you."

The smile she'd already fallen in love with lighted his face. "Thank the lord. I haven't come in my pants since I was a teenager, but it was a close thing, babe. A very close thing."

"Oh." The things he said, and how he said them, never ceased to stupefy her. She was still considering the image he'd evoked with his words when Gabe scooped her up in his arms and started across the floor. She held on tight, charmed by the gallantry. This was another thing, like fogged windows, that she thought only happened in books.

"Sunburn okay?" he asked. He wasn't even straining to hold her weight.

She sighed, totally enamored of his strength. "What sunburn?"

Gabe laughed, a sound filled with masculine satisfaction and triumph—wholly male, hotly sexual.

Rather than put her on the bed, he stood her beside it, and with no fanfare at all, caught the hem of her dress and whisked it over her head. Her arms caught in the sleeves for just a moment, making her feel awkward, but Gabe wasn't deterred. He freed her easily, then stepped back to look at her.

She still wore her sandals, was her first thought. Second was that the way he looked at her was almost tactile, like a stroke across her belly, penetrating deep to where the need rekindled and came alive once again.

Without a word Gabe kicked off his shoes as he surveyed her body. He unbuttoned his jeans, slid down the zipper and shucked both his jeans and his shorts. Lizzy was given time to look all she pleased— which was a lot. Gabe stood still for her, except to reach out with his right arm and stroke her nipples with a knuckle.

He swallowed at her continued scrutiny. "Put me out of my misery, Red. Please."

His hips were narrow in contrast to his wide chest. His abdomen was hard and flat, his navel a shallow dent surrounded by golden brown hair that felt soft to the touch. His shoulders were straight, his legs long and strong and covered in hair. His groin... She gulped, then reached out to encircle him with her hand and squeezed. So hard and so strong, his erection flexed and he made a small strangled sound. His hands fisted; his knees locked. One glistening drop of fluid appeared on the tip, fascinating her. She spread it around with her thumb, and heard his hissing breath.

"You're playing with fire, babe."

"You're so beautiful," she breathed, then started slightly when he growled and reached for her.

"Come here, Elizabeth. Let me hold you."

But as she stepped up to him he stepped forward and carried her down to the bed. Balanced on one elbow above her, he began exploring her body again.

"I love all these sexy little freckles." He traced around her breasts, skimming just below her puckered nipples, then trailed down her abdomen to her belly button. He dipped his baby fingertip there before moving over her hipbones and her upper thighs. His hand cupped her between her thighs and she groaned, knowing exactly how he could make her feel. "And this fiery red hair," he said. "I've never seen anything like it."

Elizabeth squirmed as he parted her, as one long finger pushed deeply into her.

His gaze met hers. "Does that hurt?" he asked huskily.

She shook her head. "No, please, Gabe." She spread both hands over his chest, reveling in the heat of his skin, the way his heart galloped. She loved touching his nipples and hearing his breath hitch.

"Open your legs more, Lizzy. That's it. Another finger, okay? I want to make sure you're ready, that I won't hurt you."

His words didn't make much sense to her, though she tried to listen closely. She was attuned to his scent, his touch, the warmth of his big body. She turned her face toward him to watch as her hands glided over him.

"I can't wait anymore," he growled.

Good, she thought, already so tense she ached. If she hadn't been so unused to the intimacy, she'd have demanded he get on with it, but she wasn't quite that daring yet. All she could do was try to urge him to haste with her touch.

Gabe reached for his discarded jeans and removed a condom. Curious, Lizzy stroked his body as he slipped it on, letting her palm cup him beneath his erection, where he was heavy and warm and soft. His eyes nearly closed as he groaned, and then he was over her, his entire big body shaking as he forced her legs wide and opened her with gentle fingers.

"Lizzy, look at me."

She did, snared by his beauty, by the savage hunger in his hot blue eyes. He took her in one long slow thrust and she cried out, not in pain but in incredible pleasure. Her hips lifted of their own accord, trying to make the contact as complete as possible.

Gabe slid both hands beneath her bottom and lifted her, pushing deep, retreating, pushing in again, causing the most incredible friction. "Put your legs around me, sweetheart."

She did, crossing her ankles at the small of his back, squeezing him tight. His hairy chest crushed her breasts, and she tried to rub them against him, tried to feel as much of him as she could. The sensation of him being inside her, her tender flesh stretched tight around him, was almost unbearable. The explosive feelings began building again and she struggled toward them, her head tipped back, her eyes squeezed closed.

But then Gabe cursed and paused for one throbbing heartbeat. With another muttered oath he lowered himself to her completely, opened his mouth on her throat and began thrusting hard and fast, his groan building, his body rock hard and vibrating, and Lizzy held him, enthralled as he came. She forgot her own needs, satisfied to smooth her hands over his damp back, through his silky soft hair and straining shoulders.

Gabe relaxed against her, breathing deep, his arms keeping her close, her legs still around him. After several minutes he muttered against her throat, "Sorry."

Lizzy kissed his shoulder. "For what?"

"For leaving you." He leaned up and looked at her and there was a deeply sated expression to his eyes, a tenderness that went bone deep. "I'll make it up to you in just a little bit."

Elizabeth smiled and touched his face. "I'm fine."

"I want you better than fine," he said, and he kissed her, a long, slow, leisurely kiss. He didn't seem in any hurry to stop kissing her. After a while he sat up to remove the condom—another first for her! Without much talking he carried her into the bathroom where they both soaked in a cool tub. Gabe made her wild with the way he bathed her, stroked her, teased her. After that, he seemed insatiable.

She could barely keep her eyes open after two more climaxes and a lot of new firsts, but when he settled into the bed with her, she found the foresight to ask, "Are you staying all night?"

"Yes." He pulled her to his side and pressed her head to his shoulder.

His assumption that he was welcome amused her, but then, she wanted him to stay. "Shouldn't you tell someone where you are so they won't worry?"

"I'm twenty-seven years old, sweetheart. I don't have to account for myself to my brothers."

"What about Honey? Will she worry?"

He went still, then cursed softly. "Don't move." He padded naked from the bed into the kitchen where her only phone hung on the wall. After a few seconds she heard him say, "I won't be home tonight."

There was a pause. "Yeah, well, I thought Honey might—" He laughed. "That's what I figured. See ya tomorrow."

He came back to bed and settled himself. "You were right. Sawyer said she would have worried." He kissed her forehead and within seconds he was breathing deeply.

Elizabeth stroked his chest, wondering how often he spent the night with women, if this meant anything to him at all, if she had the right to hope he'd stay with her whenever possible.

It was a long time before she, too, dozed off. But thinking of Gabe and how strong and independent and capable he was only served to slant her dreams with miserable comparisons of all the things he was, and all the things she wasn't.

And sometime in the middle of the night, the nightmares returned.

10

GABE WAS generally a sound sleeper, but then, contrary to popular belief, he seldom had a very sexy, very warm woman cuddled up to his side when he slept. Because he lived with his brothers, and because his nephew, Casey, was there, he hadn't made a habit of flaunting his social life. Having Lizzy at his side was a unique and pleasant experience.

And while he'd had no problem sleeping, he was never at any moment unaware of her curled against him.

When her skin grew warmer and her breathing deeper, he stirred. She mumbled something in her sleep and he turned his head to look at her, making a soft, soothing sound. Her hand suddenly fisted against his chest, and her head twisted from side to side.

Frowning, Gabe came up on one elbow. *"Lizzy?"* She didn't answer him. He touched her cheek and felt it wet with tears. His heart pounded. "Hey, come on, sweetheart. Talk to me."

In the dim moonlight filtering through the curtains, he could barely make out her features. He saw her mouth move, crying soundlessly, then heard a small whimper, and another, each gaining in volume.

"Lizzy?" Gabe held her closer and stroked her hair.

"You're dreaming, sweetheart. Wake up." He made his voice deliberately commanding, unable to bear her unconscious distress.

Suddenly her body went rigid as if she'd just suffered a crushing physical pain. She screamed, harsh, tearing sounds that echoed around the silent bedroom. Her arms flailed wildly and she hit him in the chest, fighting against him, against herself. Gabe pinned her arms down and rolled her beneath him.

"Wake up, Lizzy!"

Sobbing softly, she opened her eyes and stared at him. For one instant she looked lost and confused, her eyes shadowed, then she crumbled. Gabe turned to his side and held her face to his throat. "It's all right. It's all right, sweetheart."

She clutched him, and his heart broke at her racking cries. Gabe felt his eyes get misty and crushed her even closer, wanting to absorb her pain, to somehow be a part of her so he could carry some of her emotional burden.

Long minutes passed before she finally quieted, only suffering the occasional hiccup or sniff. Gabe kissed her temple, then eased her away from him. He kept the lights off and said, "Don't move, baby. I'm going to go get you a cool cloth."

He was in and out of her bathroom in fifteen seconds. When he walked in, Lizzy was propped up in the bed blowing her nose. She had her knees drawn up to her chest, the sheet wrapped around her. The first thing she said was, "I'm sorry."

"Don't make me turn you over my knee when you're already upset." Gabe scooted into bed beside her and manfully ignored the way she tried to inch away from him. He caught her chin and turned her face, then gently stroked her with the damp washcloth. "You have no reason to be sorry, Lizzy. Everyone has bad dreams every now and again."

A long silence threatened to break him and then she muttered, "It wasn't a dream."

Gabe propped his back against the headboard and handed the washcloth to Lizzy. She pressed it over her swollen eyes. Utilizing every ounce of patience he possessed, Gabe waited.

Finally she said, "I'm a little embarrassed."

"Please don't be." He kept his voice soft but firm. "I'm so glad I was here with you." His arm slipped around her shoulders and she didn't fight him as he pulled her close. "I care about you, Lizzy. Will you believe that?"

She nodded, but said, "I don't know."

Rubbing his hand up and down her bare arm, he asked, "Is it so strange for someone to care about you, sweetheart?"

"Someone like you, yes."

"What about someone not like me?"

She went still. "There's...things about me you don't know."

Gabe tightened his hold, anticipating her reaction. "You mean the awful way your mother died?"

As he'd predicted, she jerked and almost got away from him. "What do you know about that?"

"I read the articles you saved."

"How dare you!" She struggled against him, but Gabe held her tight.

"Quit fighting me, honey. I'm not letting you go." Probably not ever. It was several seconds before she went rigid against him. Gabe could feel her hurt, her anger. But he wanted to get past it, and the only way he saw to do that was to force his way. He spread his fingers across the back of her head and kept her pressed to his shoulder. "That's why you're so all-fired determined to understand this nonsense about heroism, right?"

She shuddered, and another choking sob escaped her before she caught herself. "You...you can't understand. You aren't like me. You saw a way to help and you instinctively acted. I...I let my mother die." Her hands curled into his shoulders, her nails biting, but Gabe would have gladly accepted any pain to help her. "Oh, God. I let her die."

Unable to bear it, Gabe pressed his face into her neck and rocked her while she continued talking.

"We were in a car wreck. I...I was changing the radio station trying to find a song Mom and I could sing to. We did that all the time, playing around, just having fun. It was raining and dark. Mom told me to turn the radio down, and I started to, but then the car hit a slick spot and started sliding."

Her voice had an eerie, faraway quality to it. Gabe wondered how many times, and to how many people, she'd given this guilty admission. The thought of her as a twelve-year-old child, awkward and shy, suffering what no child should ever suffer, made him desperate with the need to fix things that were years too distant to repair.

"The car went off the road and hit a tree. Mom's

door was smashed shut, the windshield broken. She was...bleeding. I thought she was dead and I just screamed and got out of the car and crouched down on the gravel and the mud, waiting and numb. Too stupid to do what I should have done."

"Oh, Lizzy." Gabe kissed her temple, her ear. He murmured inanities, but she didn't seem to hear him.

"The nearest telephone was only two miles away. If...if I'd gone for help...she'd have lived if only I hadn't frozen, if I hadn't become a useless lump crying and waiting to be helped when I was barely hurt." Her hand fisted and thumped once, hard, against his shoulder. "She was pinned in that damn car unconscious and bleeding to death and I just let her die." Sobbing again, her tears soaking his neck, she whispered, "By the time another car came by and found us...it was too late."

Keeping her in the iron grip of his embrace, Gabe reached for the lamp and turned the switch. Lizzy flinched away from the harshness of it, but Gabe was so suffused with pity, with pain and mostly with anger, he refused to let her hide. Her ravaged face was a fist around his heart, but he never wavered in his determination. Forcing her to meet his gaze, he said, "You were twelve goddamned years old! You were a child. How in the hell can you compare what a child does to a grown man?"

She looked stunned by his outrage. "I was useless."

"You were in shock!"

"If I'd reacted..."

"No, Lizzy. There is no going back, no starting over. All any of us can do is make the most of each day. You're such an intelligent woman, so giving and sincere, why can't you see that you were an innocent that day?"

"You...you said you read the articles."

"And I also know how the damn media can slant things deliberately to get the best story. One more human death means little enough to them when people pass away every day, some in more horrific circumstances than others. But a human-interest story on a young traumatized girl, well, now, that's newsworthy. You were a pawn, sweetheart, a sacrifice to a headliner. That's all there is to it."

"I let her die," she said, but she sounded vaguely uncertain, almost desperate to believe him.

"No." Gabe pulled her close and kissed her hard. "You don't know that. It was dark, it was raining. Even if, through the trauma of seeing your mother badly injured, you'd been able to run to the nearest phone, there's no guarantee that you'd have gotten there safely, that you'd have found help and they'd have made it to her in time."

She searched his face, then reached for another tissue. After mopping her eyes and blowing her nose, she admitted in a raw whisper, "My dad has said that. But I'd hear him crying at night, and I'd see how wounded he looked without my mother."

Gabe cupped her tear-streaked cheeks, fighting his own emotions. "He still had you." He wobbled her head, trying to get through to her, trying to reach her. "I know he had to be grateful for that."

Her smile trembled and she gave an inelegant sniff. "Yes. He said he was. My father is wonderful."

Relief filled him that at least her father hadn't blamed her. The man had obviously been over-wrought with grief. Gabe couldn't begin to imagine how he'd react if something happened to Lizzy. If he ever lost her, he'd—

Gabe froze, struck by the enormity of his thoughts. He loved Lizzy! It didn't require rhyme or reason. It didn't require a long courtship or special circum-stances. He knew her, and she was so special, how could he not love her?

He touched the corner of her mouth with his thumb, already feeling his body tense with arousal and new awareness. "You're a wonderful person, sweetheart, so you deserve a wonderful dad."

Her eyes were red-rimmed, matching her nose, and her lips were puffy, her skin blotchy. Gabe thought she was possibly the most beautiful person he'd ever seen. The sheet slipped a bit, and he looked at her lush breasts, the faint sprinkling of freckles and the tantalizing peak of one soft nipple.

He tamped down his hunger and struggled to di-rect all his attention to her distress. "Will you believe me that you weren't to blame, Lizzy?"

She bit her lip, then sighed. "I'll believe you don't blame me. But facts are facts. Some people possess heroic tendencies, and some people are ineffectual. I'm afraid I fall into the latter category."

Gabe caught her hips and pulled her down so she lay flat in the bed. He whisked the sheet away. "Few people," he said, while eyeing her luscious body, "are ever given the opportunity to really know if they're heroic or not." He placed his palm gently on her soft white belly. "Personally, I don't think you can judge yourself by what a frightened, shy, injured twelve-year-old did."

She stared at his mouth, firing his lust. "That's...that's why I'm studying this so hard. I want to help other adolescents to understand their own limitations, to know that they can't be completely blamed for qualities they don't possess. We're all individuals."

"And you don't want any other child to hurt as you've hurt?"

Her beautiful eyes filled with tears again. "Yes."

"I love you, Lizzy."

Her eyes widened and she stared. Stock-still, she did no more than watch him with wary disbelief. Gabe had to laugh at himself. He hadn't quite meant to blurt that out, and he felt a tad foolish.

Elizabeth was everything he wasn't. Serious, studious, caring and concerned. She had a purpose for her life, while he'd always been content to idle away his time, shirking responsibilities, refusing to settle down, priding himself on his freedom. She was at the top of her class, while he'd gone from one minor to another, never quite deciding on any one thing he wanted to do in his life. His time in college had been more a lark than anything else; he'd gone because it was expected. He'd gotten good grades because his pride demanded nothing less, but it had been easy and had never meant anything to him.

Lizzy would never consider letting someone like him interrupt her plans. She was goal-oriented, while he was out for fun. She'd told him that she wanted the summer with him, but she'd never even hinted that she might want more than that.

Trying to make light of his declaration—though he refused to take it back—he said, "Don't worry. I won't start writing you poetry or begging you to elope."

She blinked and her face colored, which added to her already blotchy cheeks and red nose, giving her a comical look. Gabe forced a grin and kissed her forehead. Damn, but he loved her. He felt ready to burst with it.

"Have I rendered you speechless, sweetheart?"

She swallowed hard. "Yes." Then: "Gabe, did you mean it?"

"Absolutely." He cupped her breast and idly flicked her soft nipple with his thumb until it stiffened. "How could I not love you, Lizzy? I've never known anyone like you. You make me laugh and you make me hot and you confuse my brain and my heart."

She scrunched up her mouth, trying not to laugh. "How...romantic."

Gabe shifted, settling himself between her long slender thighs. "I'm horny as hell," he admitted in a growl, letting her feel the hardness of his body. "How romantic did you expect me to be?"

She looped both arms around his neck and smiled. "Thank you, Gabe."

"For what?"

"For making me feel so much better." Her fingers caressed his nape, and she wound her legs around him, holding him, welcoming him. "For being here with me now, for saying you love me."

He started to reassure her that he hadn't said the words lightly, that he meant them and felt them down to his very soul. But he held back. Similar words hadn't crossed her lips, and he needed time to get himself together, to sort out this new revelation. So all he said was, "My pleasure," and then he kissed her, trying to show her without words that they were meant for each other whether she knew it yet or not.

He felt as if his life hung in the balance. He needed her, but he didn't know if he could make her need him in return.

SAWYER STOOD behind him, leaving a long shadow across the planks of wood that extended over the lake. Gabe didn't bother to turn when he asked, "You want something, Sawyer?"

"Yeah. I want to know why you're mangling all those nails."

Gabe looked at the third nail he'd bent trying to hammer it into the new dock extension he was building for his brother Morgan. Normally he did this kind of work without thought, his movements fluid, one nail, one blow. Over the years he'd built so many docks, for his family and for area residents, that he should have been able to do it blindfolded. But he'd hit his damn thumb twice already and he was rapidly make a mess of things.

In a fit of frustration he flung the hammer onto the shore and stomped out of the water, sloshing the mud at his feet and sending minnows swimming away. Sawyer handed him a glass of iced tea when he got close enough.

"From Honey?"

"Yeah." Sawyer stretched with lazy contentment. "She was all set to bring it to you herself, but I figured you might not welcome her mothering right now, since you've been a damn bear all week."

Gabe grunted in response, then chugged the entire glassful, feeling some of it trickle down the side of his mouth and onto his heated chest. "Thanks."

Sawyer lowered himself to the dry grass and picked at a dandelion. He wore jeans and nothing else, and Gabe thought it was a miracle Honey had let him out of her sight. Ever since she'd announced her pregnancy three weeks ago, Sawyer had been like a buck in rutting season. When Honey was within reach, he was reaching for her, and there was a special new glow to their love. Honey wallowed in her husband's attentions with total abandon. It was amusing—and damn annoying, because while their marriage grew visibly stronger every day, Gabe watched the time slip by, knowing Lizzy would be heading back to school soon. Three and a half weeks had passed, and he was no closer to tying her to him than he had been when he'd met her. Not once had she told him how she felt about him, yet their intimacy had grown until Gabe couldn't keep her out of his mind. He had one week left. One lousy week.

It put him in a killing mood.

Cursing, he looked at the clouds, then decided he might as well make use of Sawyer's visit, since it was obvious that's what Sawyer intended by seeking him

out. He looked at his oldest brother and said grimly,
"I'm in love."

Sawyer's smile was slow and satisfied. "I figured
as much. Elizabeth Parks?"

"Yeah." Gabe rubbed the back of his neck, then
sent a disgruntled glance at the half completed dock.
"I might as well give up on this today. My head isn't
into it."

"Morgan'll understand. He's not in a big hurry for
the dock, and we've got plenty of room to keep the
boat at the house. Besides, he suffered his own black
moods before Misty put him out of his misery."

"But that's just it." Gabe dropped down beside
Sawyer and stretched out in the sun. The grass was
warm and prickly against his back, and near his right
ear, a bee buzzed. "I don't see an end in sight for my
particular brand of misery. Lizzy is going back to
school. I've only got a few more days with her."

"Have you told her you love her?"

"Yep. She was flattered." Gabe made a wry face
and laid one forearm over his eyes. "Can you believe
that crap?"

A startled silence proved that wasn't exactly what
Sawyer had been expecting to hear. Compared to the
way he and Morgan had fought the notion of falling
in love, it was no wonder Sawyer was taken off
guard.

"You've only known her a few weeks, Gabe."

"I knew I loved her almost from the first." He lowered his arm to stare at his brother. "It was the
damnedest thing, but she introduced herself, then
proceeded to crawl right in under my skin. And I like

it. It's making me nuts thinking about her going off to college again, this time with the knowledge that she's sexy and exciting and that plenty of men will want her. She hadn't known that before, you know. She thought she was too plain, and it's for certain she was too quiet, too intense. But now..."

"Now you've corrupted her?"

Gabe couldn't hold back his grin. "Yeah, she's wonderfully corrupt. It's one of the things I love most about her."

Lizzy was the absolute best sex partner he'd ever had. Open, wild, giving and accepting. When she'd said she wanted to experience it all, she hadn't been kidding. Gabe shivered with the memory, then suffered through Sawyer's curious attention. No way would he share details with his brother, but then, there was no way Sawyer would expect him to.

And just as special to Gabe were the quiet times when they talked afterward. He'd shared stories about his mother with her, and in turn Lizzy had told him about her childhood before the accident. Their mothers were exact opposites, but both loving, both totally devoted to their children.

She'd cried several times while talking about her mom, but they were bittersweet tears of remembrance, not tears of regret or guilt. Gabe sincerely hoped she'd gotten over her ridiculous notion that she'd somehow held responsibility for her mother's death. He couldn't bear to think of her carrying that guilt on her slender shoulders.

"How much longer will she be in school?" Sawyer asked.

"Depends." Gabe sat up and crossed his forearms over his knees, staring sightlessly at the crystal surface of the lake. The lot Morgan had chosen to build on was ideal, quiet and peaceful and scenic. But Gabe preferred the bustle of the bait shops, the boat rentals, the comings and goings of vacationers. He'd always loved summer best because it was the season filled with excitement and fun on the lake. He'd invariably hated to see it coming to an end, but never more so than now, when the end meant Lizzy would leave him.

"Depends on what?" Sawyer pressed.

"On what she decides to do. She could easily graduate this semester and be done, but knowing Lizzy she may well want to further her education. She's so damn intelligent and so determined to learn as much as she can."

"We have colleges closer that she could transfer to."

"She's never mentioned doing that." It took him a moment to form the words, and then Gabe admitted, "I don't want to get in her way. I don't want to lure her into changing her plans for me, when I don't even have any plans. I've spent my whole life goofing off, while Lizzy is the epitome of seriousness." He met his oldest brother's gaze and asked, "What right do I have to screw with her life when my own is up in the air?"

Sawyer was silent a moment, and just as Gabe started to expect a dose of sympathy, Sawyer made an obnoxious sound and shook his head. "That is the biggest bunch of melodramatic bull I've ever heard uttered. You don't want to get in her way? Hell, Gabe, how can loving a woman get in her way?"

"She has plans."

"And you don't? Oh, that's right. You said you've screwed around all your life. So then, that wasn't you who helped Ceily rebuild after the fire at her restaurant? And it wasn't you who worked his butt off for Rosemary when her daddy was sick and she needed help at the boat docks? I doubt there's a body in town who you haven't built, repaired or renovated something for."

Gabe shrugged. "That's just idle stuff. You know I like working with my hands, and I don't mind helping out. But it's not like having a real job. I can still remember how appalled Lizzy was when she first came here and found out I wasn't employed. And rightfully so."

"I see. So since you don't have an office in town and a sign hanging off your door, you're not really employed?"

Gabe frowned, not at all sure what Sawyer was getting at. "You know I'm not."

Sawyer nodded slowly. "You know, when I first started practicing medicine, a lot of the hospital staff in the neighboring towns claimed I wasn't legitimate. I worked out of the house so I could be near Casey, and there's plenty of times when I don't charge someone, or else I get paid with an apple pie and an invitation to visit. It used to steam me like you wouldn't believe, that others would discount what I did just because I didn't take on all the trappings."

Gabe scowled. "It's not at all the same thing.

You're about the best doctor around." Then anger hit him and he asked, "Who the hell said you weren't legitimate?"

"It doesn't matter now."

"The hell it doesn't. Who was it, Sawyer?"

Laughing, Sawyer clapped him on the shoulder. "Forget it. It was a long time ago and what they thought never mattered a hill of beans to me. And now I have their respect, so I guess I proved myself in the end. But the point is—"

"The point is that someone insulted you. Who was it?"

"Gabe. You're avoiding the subject here, which is *you*." Sawyer used his stern, big-brother voice, which Gabe waved away without concern. He was too old to be intimated by his oldest overachiever brother. Sawyer didn't mind now that he had Gabe's attention again. "The point is, you damn near make as much money as I do, just by doing the odd job and always being available and being incredibly good at what you do. If it bothers you, well, then, rent a space in town and run a few ads and—" Sawyer snapped his fingers "—you're legitimate. An honest-to-goodness self-employed craftsman. But don't do it for the wrong reasons. Don't make the assumption that it matters to Elizabeth, because she didn't strike me as the type to be so shallow."

"She's not shallow!"

Just as Gabe had ignored Sawyer's annoyance, Sawyer ignored Gabe's. "I have a question for you."

"You're getting on my nerves, Sawyer."

"Have you let Elizabeth know that you'd like

things to continue past the summer? Or is she maybe buying into that awesome reputation of yours and thinking you want this just to be a summer fling?"

The rustling of big doggy feet bounding excitedly through the grass alerted Sawyer and Gabe that they were being joined, and judging by the heavy footsteps following in the wake of the dog, they knew it was Morgan and his massive but good-natured pet, Godzilla. Gabe twisted to see his second-oldest brother just as Morgan snarled, "Let me guess. Sawyer is giving you advice on your love life now, too?"

"Too?" Gabe lifted a brow, then had to struggle to keep Godzilla from knocking him over. The dog hadn't yet realized that he was far too big for anyone's lap. Gabe shoved fur out of his face, dodged a wet tongue and asked, "Sawyer gave you advice?"

"Hell, yes." Then: "Godzilla, get off my brother before you smother him." Morgan threw a stick into the lake and Godzilla, always up for a game, scrambled the length of the half-built dock and did a perfect doggy dive off the end. All three men watched, then groaned, knowing they'd get sprayed when Godzilla shook himself dry.

"That damn dog has no fear," Morgan grumbled.

Gabe made a face. "He must get that from you."

Morgan returned his attention to Gabe. "Sawyer fancies himself an expert on women just because Honey walks around with a vacuous smile on her face all the time."

Sawyer's grin was pure satisfaction. "Just because Misty prefers to give you hell instead—"

"She gives me hell because she loves getting me

riled." Morgan chuckled. "She claims I'm a wild man when I'm riled."

Gabe muttered, "You're always a wild man," then had to jump out of the way when Godzilla ran to Morgan and dropped the stick at his feet. Morgan was wearing his uniform, but the shirt was unbuttoned and his hat was gone. He quickly threw the stick again, this time up the hill toward the house and dry land.

"So what's the answer here, Gabe? Does your little redheaded wonder know you're in this for the long haul?"

Sawyer leaned around Gabe to see Morgan. "He told her he loved her."

Morgan raised a brow. "Is that so?"

Gabe wanted to punch them both, but instead he muttered a simple truth. "She's never returned the sentiment."

"Hm." Morgan and Sawyer seemed to be putting their collective brains together on that one until Morgan's cell phone beeped. He took it off his belt and flipped it open. "Sheriff Hudson." He grinned, and his voice changed from official to intimate. "Hi, babe. No, I'm just trying to straighten out Gabe's love life. Seems he's not going to finish my dock until I do." Morgan waited, then said, "Okay, I'll tell him."

To Gabe's disgust and Sawyer's amusement, Morgan made a kissing sound into the phone, then closed it and clipped it on his belt. "That was Misty."

Sawyer laughed outright. "I never would have guessed."

"Gabe, it seems your little woman is headed over

to see Jordan, only Jordan told Misty he had to make a house call for an injured heifer and would be away from the office for a bit. Jordan wants you to go over and make his apologies for him."

Sawyer looked at Gabe. "Why is Elizabeth hanging around with Jordan?"

With obvious disgruntlement in every line of his body, Gabe shoved himself to his feet. "Lizzy has some harebrained notion that Jordan is different, somehow nicer than the rest of us."

Morgan and Sawyer looked at each other, then burst out laughing. Gabe ignored them and snatched up his dirt- and sweat-stained T-shirt before Godzilla could step on it. Sitting on a large rock, he shoved his feet into his unlaced sneakers. His brothers were still laughing. "It's not that funny," he told them, then grinned when Godzilla threw himself into Morgan's lap, his tongue hanging in doggy bliss. Morgan made a face, resigned, and rubbed the dog's shaggy ears.

Sawyer wiped his eyes, damp from his mirth. "Elizabeth doesn't know Jordan very well, does she?"

"If you mean, has she ever seen his temper," Gabe asked, "the answer is no. I got the feeling she doesn't think Jordan *has* a temper."

Morgan choked, but there was admiration and pride in his voice when he said, "Jordan is so damn sly. He hides it well. Most women don't realize that he's only civilized on the outside."

"As long as you don't mess with his animals, or anyone he cares about, he keeps it together. But get him on one of his crusades..." Sawyer shook his head in wonder at the way his middle brother could handle himself when provoked.

Even Gabe grinned at that. Jordan gave the impression of a quiet peacemaker—and to some extent, he was. But when quiet tactics didn't work, he was more than capable of resorting to what would. "He does seem to like championing the underdog, doesn't he?"

Morgan stroked Godzilla's wet back. "Literally."

After yanking on his shirt, Gabe faced his brothers. He had his hands on his hips and a nervous chip on his shoulder. "I'm going to ask Elizabeth to give us a chance. I'm going to tell her how things'll be." He pointed an accusing finger at both of them. "But if this backfires on me, I'm coming back and kicking both your asses."

As Gabe strode away, Sawyer yelled, "Good luck."

Morgan muttered loud enough for Gabe to hear, "Never thought I'd see the day when Gabe would have women troubles."

Gabe sincerely hoped today wasn't the day, either, because he just didn't know what he'd do without Ms. Elizabeth Parks in his life.

GABE FOUND LIZZY pacing outside the front of Jordan's clinic. Her hands were clasped together, her expression frightened. Not knowing what had happened, Gabe left his car in a hurry and trotted toward her. Lizzy looked up, saw him and relief flooded her entire being.

She ran to him. "Gabe, something's wrong!"

Gabe reached for her shoulders, but she pulled away and sprinted toward the clinic door. "Listen to the animals. They're never that noisy. They're all making a racket."

Gabe could hear the whine of dogs, the screech of cats. He frowned. "Jordan always keeps them calm, but Jordan isn't here."

Lizzy put her hands to her mouth. "Something's wrong. I just know it."

Gabe considered her worry for only two seconds, then said, "Okay, just hang on, hon. I'm going in."

"How?"

For an answer, Gabe picked up a rock and tapped the glass out of a window. The howling and crying became louder with the window open—and then they smelled the smoke.

"Oh, God." Gabe jerked off his shirt, wrapped it around his hand and safely removed the broken glass. "Quickly, Lizzy. I'll go in and unlock the door. Use the cell phone in my car to call Morgan. He'll send people here. Hurry."

Lizzy ran off and Gabe carefully levered himself over the windowsill. The smoke wasn't very thick yet, but he could smell the acrid stench of burning plastic and paper. Gabe ran to the door and unlocked it, then pushed it wide open. He wasn't really given a chance to see what was burning or why, not with so many animals calling for attention. He hefted the first big cage he came to and hauled it outside.

Lizzy was back. "Morgan's on his way. What can I do?"

"Just pull these cages away from the house as I bring them out."

"But there's too many of them!"

"Just do it, Red. We don't have time to talk about it." Gabe didn't know how sick the animals were, if it was safe to open the cages... He raced inside and hauled two more out. He almost tripped over Lizzy. She had a big empty cage that she was dragging over the threshold. She had to pry open the double doors before it would fit through. Gabe frowned at her. "What the hell are you doing?"

Without answering, she ran in. She opened three pens filled with cats and began carrying the cats— without the bulky cages—outside. She got several scratches for her efforts, but the empty cage she'd taken outside was quickly filled. As Gabe worked he watched her make trip after trip, occasionally repeating the process of setting up an empty cage. The animals, penned together, might hurt each other in the excitement, but they wouldn't die.

The smoke was thicker, filling the air while frantic animal growls and cries echoed off every wall. Gabe hadn't seen any signs of an actual fire, but then the smoke tended to mask things. He had enough trouble just breathing. As Gabe struggled to release an older German shepherd, he tripped over a pile of feed and went down. His head hit the edge of a metal cage, and he saw stars.

"Gabe!"

As if from a distance he heard Lizzy calling him, and panic engulfed him. Was she hurt? He tried to raise himself, but everything spun around him. And then she was there, her arm supporting his head. She coughed several times before she was able to say, "Gabe, you have to stand."

Gabe could tell she was crying, and it cut him deeply. "Lizzy?"

"Please, Gabe. Please." She tugged on him and finally he managed to get his rubbery legs to work, leaning heavily against her. Something warm ran into his right eye, and he wondered vaguely what it was before Lizzy's insistence that he move forced him to concentrate on her demands. It was slow going, the smoke so thick he couldn't see at all.

Then blessedly clean air filled his lungs and he dropped to the ground. Lizzy knelt over him, her soft hands touching his face. "Oh, my God. You're bleeding."

Gabe said, "The animals..."

Elizabeth swabbed at his face with the hem of her dress, giving him a peek at her panties as she did so. "You've got a nasty cut."

"I'll be fine," he muttered.

She ran off but she was back within seconds. "Here, hold this against your head. Can you do that, Gabe?"

She handed him a soft pad, and he realized it was from the clinic. He pressed it hard to his head to stem the flow of blood.

"Don't you dare move, Gabriel Kasper." Her voice shook, thick with smoke and, he thought, perhaps emotion. "And don't you be seriously hurt, either." He saw her wipe tears from her face with a soot-covered hand, and he tried to smile at her, but his head was pounding painfully. "I'll never forgive you if you're seriously hurt."

Before he could reassure her she was gone and a

new panic settled in. Dear God, she'd gone into the clinic! Gabe summoned all his strength to stand, to fetch her and keep her safe, and then he heard the sound of approaching sirens and knew Morgan was almost there. He'd take care of things. But Gabe was needed still; he had to help her....

Morgan's big hands settled on Gabe's shoulders. "Don't move, Gabe."

"It's just a knock on the head. Stupid cage got in my way."

Morgan pressed him down. "Damn it, I said don't move, you stubborn fool!" Speaking to someone else, Morgan said, "Go ahead. I'll take care of my brother. Get the animals out."

"Lizzy?" Already Gabe's head was starting to clear, even as a throbbing pain settled in. The sirens were blasting, not helping one bit, keeping the animals frenzied and his head pulsing. He glared at Morgan. "Get Lizzy."

"She's inside?" Morgan jerked to his feet, but at that moment Lizzy stumbled through the doorway, aided by two firemen. She had a box of mewling kittens in her arms, and she was a dirty mess. "Here she comes now."

Morgan went to her and took the box of kittens. "Sawyer was right behind me. He'll fix Gabe up good as new."

Gabe watched her lean against Morgan for just an instant, then she straightened and hurried to Gabe.

"Shh. It's all right, babe. I'm okay. I just got knocked silly." He pulled her to his side as he carefully sat up. "Morgan! Shut the damn sirens off."

Morgan barked a few orders, and one fireman rushed to do as he was told. When silence settled in, Gabe touched Lizzy's blackened face. "Are you all right?"

She wasn't listening to him. She'd spotted Sawyer and she ran to him, then practically dragged him to Gabe. He had Jordan with him, and Jordan looked frozen with shock.

"What the hell happened?" As Sawyer spoke he opened his bag and began swabbing off Gabe's face. To Lizzy he said, "Head wounds bleed like the very devil. If he's not hurt anywhere else then he should be fine."

Gabe took pity on Jordan. "I'm fine, Jordan. Go check your animals."

Jordan looked at Sawyer and got his nod of confirmation. "Looks like he'll need a few stitches, but that's all."

"Thank God." Jordan, still looking somewhat sick and so furious he could chew nails, headed for the clinic door.

An hour and a half later, everything had quieted down. There was a lot of smoke damage to the clinic, but very little had burned. It hadn't taken a large investigation to discover that a pet owner who'd come in earlier had evidently thrown a cigarette into the trash can in the bathroom. The can was metal, so other than the walls and floor in that room being singed, the damage was mostly smoke-related. It would take quite a bit of work, and a professional crew, to get everything clean again and to rid the clinic of the smell. Jordan had a strict no-smoking policy. Gabe couldn't remember ever seeing his brother look so ravaged, or so livid.

Gabe was propped up against a tree, his head bandaged, watching the proceedings with frustration since Sawyer had flatly refused to let him help out. Lizzy had continued to work with Jordan until they had every animal accounted for and loaded into covered truck beds. Luckily, not a single animal had suffered a serious injury from the small fire, but they were frightened and skittish and Jordan was using his mesmerizing voice to calm them all. He looked like hell warmed over, but his tone didn't in any way match his expression. It was lulling and easy and sank into the bones, reassuring even the most fractious animal.

Lizzy returned to Gabe's side again and again, and each time he told her he was fine. Then she'd flit off to do more work. She had to be exhausted, but she kept on. He was so damn proud of her, he could barely contain himself.

As if she'd heard his thoughts, she glanced at him, then hurried to his side. "Do you need something to drink?"

On her knees beside him, she smoothed his hair and touched his cheek. Gabe caught her hand and carried it to his mouth. "Mm. You taste like charcoal."

She grinned. "I imagine I smell like it, too." She glanced at Jordan. "Sawyer recommended he move the animals into your garage until the clinic can be cleaned. It'll take a few days. Poor Jordan. He looks devastated."

"I know how he feels." She faced him, her brow puckered in confusion, and he said, "You scared the hell out of me, Lizzy, when you ran back in there without me. For all I knew, the place was burning to the ground. I kept thinking about you getting hurt...."

"I was careful."

"But what if you'd stumbled like I did? How the hell would I have gotten you out of there?" Her expression softened, and she leaned forward to gently kiss his mouth.

"I didn't mean to worry you."

"I love you." He hadn't said it again since she'd had her nightmare, and now he couldn't keep the words contained. Her eyes widened. "What?" he asked, sounding a little sarcastic. "You thought I made it up the first time? Not a chance."

"Oh, Gabe." Tears welled in her eyes, and Gabe held his breath, waiting to see what she would say.

Then Jordan appeared, and he hauled Lizzy to her feet. "I've been so busy trying to see to things, I haven't even thanked you yet."

Jealousy speared through Gabe as he watched Jordan lift Lizzy onto her tiptoes and kiss her soundly. She blushed, but she didn't pull away.

"This is going to be inconvenient as hell for a few days," Jordan said, hugging her tight, "but at least all the animals are safe."

Lizzy finally pulled back. She smiled and started to say, "Gabe's the real..." but then her words tapered off and she put a hand over her mouth.

Jordan raised a brow. "Real what? Hero? I'd say

you both are. Not only did you get all twenty-three animals outside, you even managed to get my baby brother out with only a knock to his hard head. That took a lot of guts, sweetheart, and I want you to know how much I appreciate it."

After Jordan walked away, Gabe took pity on Lizzy and tugged her down beside him. She was mute, her dirty face blank. Gabe kissed her ear. "How's it feel to be a heroine? Will you add your own experiences to your thesis?"

She blinked owlishly at him. "But I didn't..."

"Didn't what?" He smoothed a long red sooty curl behind her ear. "Didn't risk your life for those animals? Didn't face injury without a thought? Didn't do what had to be done almost by instinct?"

"But..." She sucked in a deep breath. "I was so scared."

"For yourself?"

She stared into his eyes, bemused. "No, not at first. I was afraid for you, and for the poor animals. But now I'm shaking with nerves." She held out her hand to show him, and Gabe cradled it in his large hand.

"Only a fool wouldn't react after going through something like this. You think after that boating incident I wasn't something of a wreck?"

"You said you weren't afraid."

"I was mad as hell at that fool for falling out of his boat. I wanted to tear something apart, and since I couldn't get hold of him, I punched a hole in my wall, then had to repair it." He gave her a sheepish grin. "It's all just reaction. Anger, fear... I've even seen people start laughing and not be able to stop. You're trembling. I got violent. We're the same, sweetheart, but we're also different. And what you did today is no less significant than what I did a year ago."

She seemed to consider that for a long time, and Gabe was content to hold her. Finally, without quite looking at him, she said, "I don't want to be a coward, Gabe."

"You're not."

She bit her bottom lip. "Have you enjoyed spending your time with me these last few weeks?"

His heart started pounding. His palms got damp. Gabe didn't give away his reaction when he answered, keeping his tone mild. "I told you I love you. So of course I love spending time with you."

She nodded slowly, then curled tighter to his side, keeping her face tucked under his chin. "How many women have you loved?"

Wrapping a red curl around his finger, he said, "Hm. Let's see. There's my mother. And now Honey and Misty."

She punched his ribs. "No, I mean romantically."

"Just you, sweetheart."

"You've never told another woman that you loved her?"

"No. Though plenty of women have told *me* that."

She was so surprised, she leaned back to glare at him. "Really?"

Gabe flicked the end of her nose. "Really. Just not the one woman I wish would tell me."

She swallowed hard. Her blue eyes were round and filled with feminine daring. Gabe held his breath.

"What would you think," she asked slowly, "of me finishing school and coming back here to stay?"

Afraid to move, Gabe said, "Are you considering doing that?"

"I think, since you love me, and since I love you, it'd make sense."

He let his breath out in whoosh. "You little witch!" He laughed and squeezed her, then winced as his head pounded. "Why haven't you told me before now?"

"I wasn't sure if I'd dreamed it or if you'd want me around forever. I wasn't sure if I was making too much of things. I'm not very good at figuring out this whole romantic business. But I do love you. I can't think of much besides you."

Going for broke, Gabe said, "You know you'll have to marry me." He frowned at her just to let her know he was serious. "You can't tell a man you love him and then not marry him."

Her face lit up and her smile was radiant, despite the black soot on her cheeks and the end of her nose. "I have to finish out my semester first. But that won't be too long."

"I can wait. I don't want you to give up anything for me." Then he shook his head. "I take that back. I want you to give up your guilt. And your free weekends because I'll be coming to see you whenever you're off school. And I most definitely want you to give up any thoughts of other men, or—"

She touched his face. "Okay."

Gabe grinned so hard his head hurt. "I just love an agreeable woman."

_____ Epilogue _____

"QUIT LOOKING so disgruntled."

Gabe frowned at Jordan, his face red, his fists clenched. "I can't believe you stole her right out from under my nose."

"She came to me willingly, Gabe. And besides, I need her."

"So do I!"

Jordan shrugged indifferently. "You can get anyone to answer your damn phones, but Elizabeth has the touch. The animals love her. More than they love me, sometimes, and that's a truth that hurts."

Gabe looked at his wife, all decked out in snowy white, her beautiful red hair hanging in long curls down her back. He wanted to get the damn reception over with so he could get her alone.

"Uh, Gabe, your lust is showing."

Gabe considered flattening his brother, but then he saw Lizzy smile and she looked so happy, he knew he had to give in gracefully. "All right, so she can be your assistant. I guess I can hire someone else." He had taken Sawyer's advice and opened a shop in town. He had more business than he could handle, but he enjoyed it so he wasn't complaining. He'd thought Lizzy would work with him, but she'd opted to sign on with Jordan, and he had to admit she had a way with animals.

She was so special she made his heart swell just looking at her.

"So magnanimous," Jordan uttered dryly. "I had no idea you had these caveman tendencies."

"I didn't, either, until I met Lizzy."

"She got a fantastic grade on her thesis. Did she tell you she's been approached about adding it to a text?"

Gabe scowled. "She's my wife. Of course she told me."

Jordan laughed, then quickly held up both hands. "All right, all right. Quit breathing fire on me. I'm sorry I mentioned it."

Thank God she'd kept his name anonymous, Gabe thought, disgruntled by the instant popularity of her *Mystique of Heroes.* He snorted. What a stupid subject. But evidently not everyone thought so; Lizzy had received several calls from men wanting her to interview them. Gabe would have liked to hide her away somewhere, but watching her bloom was a distinct pleasure, so he put up with all the other men ogling her and tamped down his jealousy.

After all, she'd married him.

Jordan nudged him with his shoulder. "She's getting ready to throw the bouquet. This always cracks me up the way the women fight over it."

Ready to get back a little of his own, Gabe said, "I noticed all those women lining up are eyeing you like a side of beef. You'll be next, you know."

Jordan shook his head, then downed the rest of his drink. "You can forget that right now. I'm rather partial to my bachelor ways."

"You just haven't met the right woman yet. When

you do, I bet you get knocked on your ass so quick
you won't know what hit you."

Jordan was ready to refute that when suddenly the
women all started shouting. He and Gabe looked up
to see that Lizzy had thrown the bouquet, but her aim
was off. It came sailing across the room in a dramatic
arch. Right toward Jordan.

He almost dropped his drink he was so surprised,
but when the flowers hit him in the chest, he managed to juggle everything, and was left standing there
holding the flowers.

Gabe laughed out loud, Lizzy covered her mouth
with a hand to stifle her giggles and Jordan, seeing a
gaggle of women rushing toward him, muttered,
"Oh, hell."

Gabe looked at his wife and winked, then whispered to Jordan, "You better make a run for it."

And he did.

Gabe smiled as Lizzy headed toward him, looking
impish and beautiful and so sexy he decided the reception was well and truly over. He kissed her as
soon as she reached him, then whispered against her
lips, "That was a dirty trick to play on my brother."

She grinned. "I was tired of all the women here
looking at you with broken hearts. It's time for Jordan
to be the sacrificial lamb."

Gabe shook his head with mock sympathy.
"Damn, I feel sorry for him."

Startled, Elizabeth leaned into his side and asked,
"Why?"

Taking her by surprise, Gabe hoisted her up in his
arms, which left her delicate white gown loose

around her legs, giving everyone a sexy peek. Over the sound of the raucous applause from all the attending guests, Gabe whispered, "Because the prettiest, sexiest, smartest female is already taken—and I have her."

Elizabeth laughed. "You are a charmer, Gabe."

He started out of the room, holding her close to his heart. Right before he disappeared through the doorway, he looked up and saw Jordan backed against a wall, women surrounding him. Gabe shook his head.

He wished his only single brother all the same love that he'd just found.

The women looked determined enough to see that he got it.

HARLEQUIN® *Temptation.*

Buckhorn County, Kentucky, may not have any famous natural wonders, but it *does* have the unbeatable Buckhorn Brothers. Doctor, sheriff, heartthrob and vet—all different, all irresistible, all larger than life.

There isn't a woman in town who isn't in awe of at least one of them.

But somehow, they've managed to hang on to their bachelor status. Until now...

Lori Foster presents:

Sawyer
#786, On Sale June 2000

Morgan
#790, On Sale July 2000

Gabe
#794, On Sale August 2000

Jordan
#798, On Sale September 2000

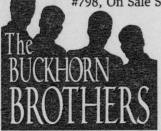

The BUCKHORN BROTHERS

All gorgeous, all sexy, all single. *What a family!*

If you enjoyed what you just read,
then we've got an offer you can't resist!

Take 2 bestselling love stories FREE!

Plus get a FREE surprise gift!

Romance is just one click away!

online book **serials**

➢ *Exclusive* to our web site, get caught up in both the daily and weekly online installments of new romance stories.

➢ Try the Writing Round Robin. Contribute a chapter to a story created by our members. Plus, winners will get prizes.

romantic **travel**

➢ Want to know where the best place to kiss in New York City is, or which restaurant in Los Angeles is the most romantic? Check out our Romantic Hot Spots for the scoop.

➢ Share your travel tips and stories with us on the romantic travel message boards.

romantic reading **library**

➢ Relax as you read our collection of Romantic Poetry.

➢ Take a peek at the Top 10 Most Romantic Lines!

Visit us online at

www.eHarlequin.com

on Women.com Networks

HARLEQUIN
Duets™

Pick up a Harlequin Duets™ from August–October 2000 and receive $1.00 off the original cover price. *

Experience the "lighter side of love" in a Harlequin Duets™. This unbeatable value just became irresistible with our special introductory price of $4.99 U.S./$5.99 CAN. for 2 Brand-New, Full-Length Romantic Comedies.

**Don't miss
an exciting opportunity
to save on the purchase of
Harlequin and Silhouette books!**

Buy any two Harlequin or
Silhouette books and save
$10.00 off future Harlequin
and Silhouette purchases

OR

buy any three
Harlequin or Silhouette books
and save **$20.00 off** future
Harlequin and Silhouette purchases.

*Watch for details
coming in October 2000!*

PHQ400